THE MALACCA CANE

The Malacca Cane

Robert Kemp

ISIS
LARGE PRINT
Oxford

First published in Great Britain 1954
by Duckworth

Published in Large Print 2001 by ISIS Publishing Ltd,
7 Centremead, Osney Mead, Oxford OX2 0ES
by arrangement with Society of Authors

British Library Cataloguing in Publication Data
Kemp, Robert, 1908-1967
    The Malacca cane. – Large print ed. – (Serendipity series)
    1. Large type books
    I. Title
    823.9'12[F]

ISBN 0-7531-6585-6 (hb)
ISBN 0-7531-6586-4 (pb)

Printed and bound by Antony Rowe, Chippenham and Reading

CONTENTS

To
META

CHAPTER
ONE

Mansie is late for
High Tea

To those of the right way of thinking, No. 2 Bleachfield is a most desirable address. In these days, when no one is pleased with anything, it is a comfort to reflect that thirty-seven human souls share it and, so far as stone and lime can satisfy, are content. At least it was thirty-seven, but babies are frequently being born, young men are in and out of the Forces, and young women marry up or down the hill, until it would be reckless to guarantee the accuracy of the figure. Indeed, one consequence of the story which I have to tell may be that it will top forty. And then some old party, a disciple of the law of averages and the equilibrium of nature, will quietly snuff out in the night, in order to bring it back to a more reasonable level.

I have encountered theorists who maintain that thirty-seven is too many for one stair. Yet listen to their rhapsodies when you point out to them some ultra-modern block, raised upon stilts by Le Corbusier and loud with the whine of automatic lifts, patent garbage chutes and duodenal ulcers! Others, of more suburban leaning, regret that "Bleachfield" sounds so plain, lacking "Crescent" or "Quadrant" after it, as they have on the new housing estates. If only such shallow critics could be brought to realise that the tenements were called "Bleachfield" for the good and sufficient reason that they were put up on the ancient bleachfield of the city, beside the Water of Leith! Does not the very baldness lend distinction?

That has always been one of Mrs Thin's favourite arguments. She was in excellent service in her young day, and retains the nose of a whippet for true distinction. She lives, with her son Mansie, in the top flat left, and on the very day when Mansie was late for high tea she had already put one or two in their place on the subject of No. 2 Bleachfield.

The more stairs one lives up, the more sensitive one naturally becomes, and Mrs Thin lived up eighty-three. So, when Mrs Bremner, of the floor below, remarked that she pitied an elderly woman the long climb, Mrs Thin took umbrage. Few will be found to blame her. Such an observation might barely be tolerated from a privileged friend who lived at the sea-level of the main door. Coming from the lady whose pulley always squeaked as you were dropping off to sleep, it savoured of impertinence.

Mrs Bremner was building up a reputation for herself on the stair of being a friendly, helpful soul. She was always inquiring after the health of her neighbours, their children, their first cousins in Macrihanish, and offering to bring back a loaf for them when she was out at the baker's. Mrs Thin thought such behaviour common, and

2

even if she had not thought it common, she was too wary to walk into the trap. She had met these kindly souls before. They are never off the doorstep until you are in real trouble. When that occurs, they vanish like snow off the dyke, murmuring of destitution or a sharp attack of double pneumonia. Mrs Thin knew that all they desired was to worm their way through the front door, to guess the price of the sitting-room curtains and to waste time drinking tea.

She had another solid reason for her determination to hold Mrs Bremner at arm's length. That daughter of hers, Myrtle Bremner, had once been such a taking wee lassie, with tight fair pigtails. Mrs Thin often saw her playing peever, or hopscotch as it is vulgarly known, with other girls on the pavement outside the tenement. That is, one day she saw her. The next she heard the staccato clip of high-heeled shoes on the stone stair. Glancing over the banisters, she saw Myrtle — no more skipping or vaulting with two hands on the rail but never missing a step — quite the young lady. And the tight-drawn strands of hair ending in ropes like marine cables — gone! In their place a soft pile that shimmered like the new diffused street lighting and turned her smooth brow and little ears into milk. A cherry-coloured ribbon bound it at the nape of her neck. That girl, Mrs Thin instantly said to herself, has been indulging in some patent shampoo! And in her heart there sounded a warning like the air-raid siren erected at Leith Docks during the recent world conflict.

Not that Mansie was a boy of that kind — at least not yet. But she had kept her eyes peeled during her fifty-

3

three summers, and often during her winters too. She could only conclude that girls like Myrtle existed for the express and annoying purpose of instilling into the minds of boys like Mansie, at an unsuitably early age, disturbing ideas which were never there before. If it had lain in her power, she would there and then have dropped an iron curtain between herself and the Bremners. But those who climb a common stair can scarcely behave as if they dwelt in bungalows. When Mrs Bremner commiserated with her one morning as she returned from work, Mrs Thin replied, in the voice one might employ to a strange and over-familiar butcher.

"Mrs Bremner, I should be the last to complain of the stairs. For one thing, the air is purer at the top — that was publicly stated by the Medical Officer of Health — and for another, the top landing enjoys a comparative privacy which Mansie and I have come to value."

"I only meant," replied Mrs Bremner, not a little put out, "that when you've been up and down half a dozen times in a day, your poor old legs must be sore and your heart pounding."

Mrs Thin refused to meet her half-way.

"Mrs Bremner," she said, "I think if you consider the health of the tenants of the top flats, you will find that it is to be envied. Take Mr Clague, across the landing from me. He has not enjoyed a day's illness in his life, unless you count the occasion on which his jaw was broken. He was confiding in me only yesterday how much he grudges his health contributions."

Leaving Mrs Bremner to ponder her words, she began to mount the stairs. On the second landing whom should she meet but Myrtle Bremner on the way out. On account of the steepness of the ascent, she was obliged to notice that Myrtle was wearing nylon stockings and a peach-coloured petticoat with scalloped edges. The almost gastric satisfaction which her encounter with Mrs Bremner had left behind, like the taste of marzipan, all of a sudden disappeared, to be replaced by the dyspeptic gnawings of anxiety.

Mrs Thin, although not a member of any organised church, was, like all natives of the Shetland Islands of her sex, a deeply religious woman who never missed a Sunday Evening Service on the wireless. She judged a sermon not according to the grandeur of the preacher or the degree of Oxford in his voice, but simply on its comfort. There are clergymen who whisk the blankets off, cold sponge in hand; others excel as tuckers up. It was to a stammering divine, later dropped by the selectors, that she wed her acquaintance with a verse of singular beauty and usefulness:

"Count your blessings, count them one by one,
And it will surprise you what the Lord hath done!"

Mrs Thin heard this by accident when Mansie was eighteen months, and she had kept it as her motto ever since. On the wall of her mind it hung, traced out in an illuminated hand and embellished with a border of roses. Whenever there was nothing else to count, except sums owing to local tradesmen, the rent collector and the insurance man, she made a practice of counting her blessings.

And now here she was, in a state almost of affluence, yet a weight dragged at her heel like a prisoner's ball and chain. Not being one to lie down under gloom, she judged it high time to tot up her blessings.

It will surprise you what the Lord hath done! Are you telling me, Mrs Thin exclaimed to herself. That was not half strong enough. A stunned amazement, an incredulous bewilderment — her feelings of pious gratitude might have been more exactly rendered in such terms.

"If you had told me when Mansie was born," she said to herself, "that I would be living in this comfortable apartment, which although not so fashionable in its situation as the grand houses of the West End of Edinburgh must stand at approximately the same altitude, I should have begged leave to doubt. Hill air is recommended by the medical profession for afflictions of the chest. As neither Mansie nor I suffer from such afflictions, that is in all probability the reason, for here we are perched on a little mountain-top. The extraordinary vitality of Mr Clague, incidentally, bears out this theory. If one lives in a town, it is best to be central, and we are only a penny fare from Princes Street, at least we should be if they had not raised it to twopence. The trams make a friendly, companionable jangle as they round the bends. They have nothing like that in the new housing schemes. There they must endure all the inconveniences of country life, and other people into the bargain. Owls hoot at them vindictively the whole night long, and blackbirds whistle of malice aforethought as soon as the sun appears. The neighbours keep hens, homing pigeons, and terriers which have not been trained to respect the public footpaths. Besides, No. 2 is so well maintained. The stair is cunningly lit at every bend, so that we are spared the invasion of courting couples."

Then she thought of Mansie, so called in loving diminutive of the good Shetland "Magnus," how he had survived convulsions, how he had narrowly missed extinction when the horse in the Co-operative milk lorry bolted, how he might have been drowned when he fell into Inverleith Pond at the age of three, but was not, thanks to the gentleman who owned the model of the *Titanic*. From a child who was always sick on buses, he had developed into a a steady young man, with his military service behind him and a foreseeable future in the head office of the Jupiter Assurance Company. It might have been better had he not taken up so cordially with the Children of Gabriel, but, as Mrs Thin reminded herself, she was reckoning the blessings — the ointment, not the flies. As usual, the Lord had surprised her with a margin in hand.

So the day wore on. Myrtle did not loom up again. In the afternoon she collected her dividend at the Co-op and invested part of it in half a dozen handkerchiefs of Belfast linen for Mansie. On her way home she hovered at a fishmonger's long enough to snap up two kippers of superior succulence. Then she returned to cook her own and Mansie's high tea, for she fed her son with a high maternal devotion, being aware that he was a pale, subdominant youth, younger and even less impressive than his twenty semi-conscious years might warrant, and that victuals might increase his personality as well as his girth.

Mrs Thin was a trifle late, and as she mounted the eighty-three steps an assortment of odours caressed her olfactory nerve, as beauty queens might compete to pet a stray kitten. What an aromatic orchestra, blending in the riposte of chords! Bat-eared musicians, they claim, can put a name to all the notes that are blared and sawed forth at one simultaneous second. So could Mrs Thin disentangle the thorough bass of cod cooking in deep fat from the brassy fanfares of sausages on the grill or fresh herring as they leaped in the pan. To this symphony finnan-haddocks, as they baked in milk, supplied their gentle flutings, and somewhere pickled beetroot cut through with the acerbity of a triangle. When she rested on the top landing to feel for her key, all these vapours swirled round her head with intoxicating bravura. She entered and prepared to vary the texture with the full, oily tone of her pair of kippers.

Mansie had never been one to keep a woman hanging about. His punctuality could be counted upon, partly because of his innate thoughtfulness and partly because of his fondness for the general weather forecast at five minutes to six. He never willingly missed one of these useful programmes. He always switched off as soon as the announcer said that the news bulletin would follow in forty seconds, but anyone who thought that he dismissed the forecast from his mind would be mistaken. If next day a roaring gale blew in from Fife on the north, he would remark to the young lady who brewed the office tea, "We were promised south-west winds, moderate to fresh." This he uttered with a suppressed smile, implying that man had not yet mastered the universe and never would, although it is doubtful if she took the point. At least she always smiled back.

Mrs Thin realised that something was amiss when she heard a man's voice babbling of troughs of low pressure and knew that one more Children's Hour had come and gone. Since the flesh of the kippers was just curling away from the bone, she had no alternative but to pop them on an ashet in the oven, well though she understood that their succulence must be the first casualty. Luckily she had not infused the tea. She stoked the fire and contemplated the vacant carpet slippers.

Mansie's foot was not heard on the stair till twenty to seven, the longest overdue he had ever been since total immersion in Inverleith Pond put him behind schedule at the age of three. Nevertheless she did not fly to the door, having an acute horror of hysterical conduct which might become the subject of comment on the stair.

When he entered, he was all in one piece, but grey.

"Sorry to be late, Ma," he said, sitting down as usual and changing into his slippers. "If you've had your tea, don't trouble about mine."

"I have kept the kippers warm," Mrs Thin replied, repelling the suggestion that she could eat alone. She served the kippers, and out of the corner of her eye watched Mansie remove the backbone of his with trembling fingers.

"What kept you?" she asked.

"I have been to the Cave Adullam."

"Is something wrong?"

Mansie laid down his knife and fork.

"It would be truer to say that nothing is right. Ma, you will have to know some day. Brother Methuselah has made off with the Glad Tidings Fund, Brother Jeroboam lies asleep in the Inner Sanctuary, the worse for liquor, and as for Sister Dinah, she will never be worth the half of a Hallelujah again. Can I have a second cup, please?"

There was no steadier pourer of a cup of tea in a crisis than Mrs Thin.

"Which finishes me with religion," said Mansie, picking a bone from the back of his throat. "Thank you. The kippers are a little dry, but doubtless that is no one's fault but my own. I don't suppose, Ma, that by any chance you heard the weather forecast?"

CHAPTER
TWO

The Children of Gabriel

Is the frog born on the day when the sun transforms the gelatinous egg into a wriggling tadpole? Or later, when his tail has shrunk to naught and he struggles ashore? The human species confronts us with a similar dilemma. The day on which an infant is thrust, protesting, from his mother's womb possesses a mere arbitrary convenience. So long as birth certificates persist, it may be inscribed upon them as well as any other. It would be quite as sensible to enter the moment at which the glint appeared in father's eye.

Mansie's legal birthday resembled the date of the frog's transition from egg to tadpole, and in the opaque ditchwater of childhood he continued to wriggle until his late teens. A frog's first moment of complete self-consciousness may well occur when his tail disappears and, perceiving that it is now or never, he strikes out for dry land. Mansie's tail did not drop off until he left Her Majesty's Forces.

Life in the ditch has all the freedom of a well-run prison or expensive school. One may shoot freely in all directions but never beyond the edge. In his tadpole stage, Mansie was never fully aware of anything. At the age of five he was scooped out of one ditch and emptied into another, called school, where there was just a sufficiency of water to swim and to breathe according to the laws of tadpoles. At the age of fifteen he was caught in a glass jar called the Jupiter Assurance, and from this, at eighteen, he was transferred to a murky, khaki tank called a barracks. All these ages are merely nominal, for he had not yet been properly born. It was in the barracks that his tail vanished. The wind is probably blowing it, black and shrivelled, about the asphalt square to this day. At the hour of his liberation he stood blinking in the sunlight beside the orderly room, which he had never fully comprehended with all his faculties till that instant.

Of course it was the global balings of the Great Powers that scooped Mansie from the Assurance jar to the Forces tank. But Mrs Thin had herself scooped him into that jar in the first place. The tadpole by its nature can recognise nothing short of a prod. Mansie, therefore, is not to be blamed if he remained in ignorance of the precarious nature of the daily existence of the Thins. Even if he had been fully sentient, he would have been hoodwinked by the great deception which Mrs Thin practised, for the sake of her own and her son's self-esteem.

Being in dire need while he was yet a child, she had snatched at the post of office cleaner as at a straw. That means six to eight-thirty every morning. But they were at starving-point.

Nevertheless she succeeded in behaving as if this kind of thing was slightly off the beaten track. She somehow conveyed the impression that high officials of Jupiter

Assurance had pertinaciously sought her services, and that out of sheer pliability she could not refrain from granting them as a favour. Within six months this impalpable emanation had won her the halo of being a woman of superior-type. That was how she was spoken of by her fellow-cleaners, and in the end even by the management itself. To such an extent that, a vacancy for a boy occurring, she was able to ingratiate Mansie into the service of the Company. He wriggled about the head office for three years, delivering mail and files and inter-departmental memoranda. He was even allowed to refill the ink-wells. When her son took up this valuable appointment, Mrs Thin, with statesmanlike vision, resigned from the service of Jupiter Assurance. Already there had grown up a race of junior clerks who did not know that Mansie's mother had washed down the front steps.

The Army could scarcely be expected to realise that Mansie was still at the pre-natal stage. The lad walked about in a dream, turned right when the sergeant-major shouted left, frequently peered down the muzzles of loaded weapons and through sheer absence of mind almost shot a major. In the end the Army had to confess defeat. After fruitless efforts at remonstrance and even punishment they tucked him away in the paymaster's office. He proved to be a reliable counter, but after all mathematics, like St Vitus Dance, is involuntary.

Mansie began to lose his tail when he noticed a potato peeling awash in a dixie of tea. This was life's physicianly slap to provoke the cry of existence. By the time he walked out past the orderly room, through the

13

whitewashed gates and on to the pavement, the iron civilian pavement, he was fully delivered. For the first time in his life he was aware that all the tramcars were painted maroon.

After the bleak architectural style of the barracks and their bare concessions to the creature comforts (it was said that the plans were intended for Poona, but were sent to Edinburgh by mistake), his delight in No. 2 Bleachfield bubbled like an underground river. Everything was better at No. 2, the tea, the porridge, the kippers, the company. Every time he lay back in bed and pulled the multicoloured patchwork quilt up to his chin, he remembered the grey army blankets in the long barrack-room, and how cold the floor smote upon the soles of the feet there, compared with his own little rug. The jangle of the trams and the creak of the spring mattress of his mother's bed, which was let into a recess in the kitchen combined to instil a glow of security into his life, like the movement of friends in another part of the house. And the motherly voices which greeted him on the stair were as the descant of angels compared with the peppery military ejaculations which he trusted to hear no more.

Those familiar with the high standards of the Jupiter Assurance Company may be astonished, even incredulous, to learn that within a fortnight Mansie was reinstated in the office, and promoted from messenger to junior clerk. But Mansie had, unknown to himself, impressed Mr Woodburn, the manager, by his docility. When it emerged that he was good at figures, he was in, for Mr Woodburn loathed all such as argued but could not multiply, a class of persons thickly populating the face of this globe. Furthermore, the city appeared to be teeming with dangerous young men all set on being manager of the Jupiter Assurance, and that before Mr Woodburn had reached the age of retirement. Someone must stay at the bottom in this life, he told himself plaintively. In Mansie he read the temperament of one not only content but relieved to remain a subordinate. He remembered, too, in the background, the exceptionally superior woman. There was no monkey business, no effluvium of book-cooking, about Magnus Thin.

Now to paint the darker side of the picture. Some could be found, even on the stair, who would say that Mansie was only half these. Mrs Bremner, in character a kindly soul, contented herself with remarking that it was a great pity about Mansie Thin and that Mrs Thin had her heartfelt sympathy. This did not go far enough for Mrs Murdoch, over whom the arcane of medicine exercised a reptilian fascination, thanks to her own precarious state. She read the medical hints in every newspaper she could lay hands on, and her opinion that perhaps Mrs Thin had married a first cousin or other near relation was not lightly propounded. Incidentally, whom had Mrs Thin married? To judge by the offspring of the union, he must have been a poor fish. Although speaking thus freely among themselves, they were fair to Mansie's face — not by complete hypocrisy, for they had watched him through the tadpole stage, pulled him out from under motor cars and exercised a general surveillance over him.

15

The only exception to this benevolence was Ned Turpin. The Turpins had the door opposite Mrs Bremner's — that is to say, they lived three up, right — and were of coarse fibre. The senior Mr Turpin worked as a bar-tender near the Foot of Leith Walk, which had shaped his character. His approach to life was marked by crude realism and was entirely wanting in delicacy or finer feeling. Ned took after his father.

He was two years older than Mansie, and eight years brawnier. He had bullied Mansie since they were able to walk. The neighbours always took the part of the weaker, but whenever the stair was empty the weaker went to the wall. Ned would kick him in the behind, twist his arms round his back till he screeched, and force him against the banisters till he almost toppled over. When Ned was called up for national service, Mansie could not understand why he was so happy. After that came his own military career, which kept him out of Ned's path for two years more. Then one day after his return he was mounting the stair when he heard a step clumping down from above. An echo of that step, swifter, lighter, sounded within and constricted the casing of his heart and lungs. He stood to the side. Ned paused and looked at him.

"Hello, you back, Skinny?"

It was a circumstance of peculiar humiliation that Ned preferred "Skinny" to "Thin." He went on:

"Bloody fine soldier you must have made! I lost a bet the day they took *you*."

It is to this Turpin that we owe the description of Mansie as "that moron." While we appreciate that this was not a polite thing to say, we cannot deny that Ned seemed to have some warrant for it. His pragmatical outlook promised him a brilliant future in the licensed trade, where his forthright judgment of character coupled with his weight and strength caused him to be in high demand as a chucker-out. Mansie never spoke to him if he could help it. He tried to tell himself that one adult does not twist another adult's arm, yet he always stood aside on the stair. It was an ingrained habit, which he had not been able to leave behind with his tail.

When Mansie first told her that he had joined the Children of Gabriel, Mr Thin worried and woke up in the small hours. Although a religious woman, and liberal rather than dogmatic in her theology, she had never heard of the Children except in a way that suggested they were beyond the pale. She had listened with profit to addresses by pontiffs of every creed and had even been much solaced by the Chief Rabbi, but she could not fail to be cognisant that the Children of Gabriel were not admitted to the microphone. In short, they were not within sight of being orthodox, and every respectable woman, who is carving a path for her offspring through this worldly wilderness, must acknowledge a predirection for the orthodox. When Mansie told her of Brother Jeroboam, she contented herself with the observation, "I cannot recall that he has ever preached on the wireless."

She had thought that this would floor Mansie — he was easily floored, the poor soul — but on the contrary he replied pat, "That is hardly to be wondered at, Ma, seeing that the B.B.C. is one of the outward and visible forms of Anti-Christ."

On another occasion she looked up from her evening paper as Mansie was doing justice to a pie and chips, and said, "You will no doubt be sorry to read that one of the Children is in disgrace."

Mansie stopped chewing, and looked up with apprehension in his eye.

"Yes. He has refused to do his military service. He has been severely reprimanded by the Conscientious Objectors' Tribunal."

"We do not call that a disgrace," Mansie answered without even having to think. "We consider that an honour, which will no doubt be worth three Hallelujahs at the Friday meeting."

Mrs Thin was amazed.

"Do you mean to tell me," she said, "that the Children of Gabriel would turn a deaf ear to the call of King and Country?"

"We acknowledge only one King, and there is only one country of which we claim to be citizens," retorted Mansie with a pitying smile that exasperated his mother.

"Would *you* have —?" She could not frame the rest of the question.

"Undoubtedly, if I had been treading the path of light. MacGill seems to be using less meat per pie these days."

And there the matter rested.

The story of conversion had been the usual one, of air — in this case hot air — rushing to fill the vacuum which nature so abhors. Sunday was always a lonely day for Mansie, because his mother divided her time between listening to wireless sermons, preparing vegetables for broth, attending the Sabbath stew with many stirs and sips, changing bed linen and performing various household tasks which her professional duties ruled out on the more customary days of the week. Mansie always had a long lie on Sunday, breakfast in bed and a late lunch. By evening he was gasping for air, and felt the need of looking about him. He would walk, not in any of the numerous green spaces provided by the Corporation, but up to Princes Street. His primary motive was to reassure himself that this important thoroughfare was still in place. Once he felt convinced upon this point, he would walk home contented. They then went early to bed.

Many examples of light behaviour forced themselves upon his attention during these rambles. Within one of the clubs, just as a liveried senitor drew the blinds, he caught sight of an elderly gentleman knocking back a tumbler half full of whisky at one gulp. Beardless youths hid in doorways and dashed out at one another, shouting "Feet, Scotland, feet!" Sometimes they leapt up to touch anything just out of reach, like the frame to support a canvas awning above a shop window. Sometimes they sang snatches of songs. They addressed remarks to strange young ladies, who instead of preserving their dignity glanced round and then went off into fits of giggles. He was not surprised, one evening, to observe Myrtle Bremner, looking flighty in a scarlet coat, participating in these scenes. He thought of mentioning this to Mrs Thin on his return, aware of her fondness for the theme of Mrs Bremner and the manner in which she brought up her children, but for some reason he did not. I shall seize the opportunity of a word with her myself on the stairs, he reflected. When he did, Myrtle only giggled worse.

Before he turned his back on Princes Street, he always paid a visit to the Mound, the Earthen Mound as it was once called, and made a grand tour of all the doctrines and philosophies that were paraded there for his inspection. He was accusing with the communists, indignant with the Scottish Nationalists, horrified with the anti-vivisectionists, appalled with Protestant Action, parched with the prohibitionists and, most memorable experience of all, damned with the Children of Gabriel. It was really this splendid sense of damnation that first drew him towards the Children. The other orators cancelled one another out, collectivism obliterating distributism, Calvin and St Thomas of Aquin wrestling till they were both spent upon the pavement, pacifism taking the sting out of patriotism, and internationalism neutralised by the manifest misdeeds of every nation, but Brother Jeroboam and the Children of Gabriel towered mighty in hell-lit isolation. So at last he ignored all the others, drawn irresistibly towards the Children, as a wandering space-ship might be attracted by the most potent planet in the nebula. Besides, there is a conspicuous importance in being damned.

Brother Jeroboam could speak for seven hours at a stretch. Since the world, the flesh and the devil, with special reference to the hereafter, were his main subjects, he need not have repeated himself once. But he was well aware that during those seven hours his audience might have changed as often as forty-two times, so that he spoke with a rotary motion. His disquisitions were like a top spinning at high speed, but so painted that it presented a constant pattern to the beholder, accompanying itself with a sonorous infernal hum. In appearance he was dark, suave and sickly. His nose, though long, was not large enough to cover his nostrils, which gaped alarmingly, like a horse's.

The first time that Mansie set eye and ear upon Brother Jeroboam, he had arrived at one of those recurring points designed to cap a spell of pleading and simultaneously to stab the conscience of the newest bystander.

"Who is on the Lord's side?" he shouted. "Who has plunged into the divine disinfectant, and emerged on the other side with a spotless certificate of decontamination? Who has put on the rubber suiting of God, proof against the radio activity and atomic blast of the Devil?"

He continued in this vein for perhaps a minute, as if giving a pep talk on supernatural air-raid precautions. All the time he eyed his audience hopefully, and implied that it might not be too much to suppose that in such a large gathering at least one would admit to being on the Lord's side. But the time was not ripe. Had anyone stepped forward at that stage, he would have been discomfited — not that anything could discomfit Brother Jeroboam for long.

"Come," he continued, "I will wrestle in prayer. I will pray that some among you may come over to the Lord's side from the marshes of sin where you have taken up your unrepentant stance."

And how he prayed! As he described the bogs and quicksands of iniquity, some began to glance down at the pavement and to wriggle their toes to see if it squelched; others moved away, as before an advancing tide. In the meantime Brother Jeroboam kept peering round as he prayed, with the vigilance of an auctioneer determined not to miss a single bid. All the time he was addressing the Lord in rapid and forceful terms.

Under the mesmeric strain, a middle-aged man, under whom the pavement had begun to quake, shifted forward six inches. Brother Jeroboam was into him in a jiffy, like a fisherman into a salmon. Breaking short his petitions to the Lord without so much as an apology, he cried:

"Ah, brother, you are welcome, step right forward! Praise the Lord, the iron curtain is breached and a black sheep has crossed the frontier! Step right forward, brother, right to the foot of the throne! Brother Gamaliel, shove back these voracious sinners and make room for the new brother! Sister Dinah! — Action stations, Sister Dinah! Yours be the honour of giving our new brother the last heave across Jordan! Lord, I thank thee for making me the unworthy instrument — ah, sir, you in the blue muffler! Join our new brother at the foot of the throne!"

One more bystander stirred, and as the first convert was gaffed, Brother Jeroboam switched on to the new victim.

"Yes, sir, the mud of sin and shame is thick on your boots — Sister Dinah, throw out the life-line! Ah, Lord, we are bountifully blessed to be the means of garnering such sheaves."

Too bemused to be sure of anything except that his boots were in a deplorable condition, the new penitent seized Sister Dinah's hand and was yanked over Jordan. The end came when out of the blue and without any preamble, Brother Jeroboam cried:

"Brother Methuselah, the collection."

At this an elderly man moved forward like a saintly whippet from the trap and began to move with supple speed among the crowd. Just as may the fisher who with the speed of lightning sweeps his net into the shoal, he caught some. The majority escaped and joined whatever group looked as if it could not possibly be sending round the hat.

It must not be thought that Mansie was won by the blandishments of Brother Jeroboam or helped over Jordan at the first or yet the twenty-first hearing. It took dour theological arguments to convince Mansie, for Mansie was much more wideawake than, for example, Brother Gamaliel, who thought that domesticity was a vice practised in pyramids by the ancient Egyptians. Despite his unexpressive exterior, Mansie had the stuff of Hume and Knox in him. And he was his mother's son.

CHAPTER
THREE

The Day of Judgment

No one could accuse Mansie Thin of being hasty; if anything, he was prudent and over-cautious to a fault. He did not care to think that any course he took might be experimental, or that he might be compelled to retrace his steps. So it was only after many Sunday evenings passed in close attention to Brother Jeroboam that he finally stepped into Jordan out of the bog of sin and shame, and was helped out on the other bank by the damp hand of Sister Dinah. How strange that those who lead exemplary lives should imagine themselves to be in such peril!

It would be idle to deny that Mansie's daily work played some part in his conversion. In this scurrying world few spare a passing thought for those who spend their days in life and industrial assurance. To the young man who enters this profession, the first words uttered are "expectation of life" and he quickly discovers that it is short. How Mansie trembled when he learned that he had only fifty-five more years to live! And before that he might be run down by a pantechnicon, dropped from a great height by a crane, blown off the Forth Bridge, wound round a pylon in an air disaster or chopped into small pieces through some trivial misunderstanding on the railway. Some of the clients of the Jupiter Assurance even succeeded in having themselves struck accurately on the head by falling chimney pots, a thought which took much of the pleasure out of a windy day. There were perils at every corner. You could not stand in a bus queue, but a drunken motorist, unlicensed, in a stolen car, would mow it down; having a pleasant dip in the swimming pool, one might take cramp and not be noticed till they drained the bath some hours later. Even if one stuck to the ordinary diseases of which everyone has heard, there was quite a variety to choose from. He spent hours attempting to decide which was the most painful and long drawn out. Such thoughts incline the human mind to gloom, and induce the young man of pensive cast to consider the state of his soul.

Nor did the wonderful improvements to the atom bomb console him. While his tidy mind could not resist a certain professional satisfaction at the idea of settling the whole business of life insurance in one day, the more leisurely methods of nature did at least permit the files to be kept up to date. The generality of the doom caused him to turn his glance outwards and to take account not only of his own inner condition, but of that displayed by his fellow-citizens. And when he thought of his fellow-citizens, he was profoundly shocked, as politicians are wont to say of events for which no one can possibly hold them responsible.

There they were, these fellow-citizens, knocking back whisky in the clubs, demanding "What's the matter with the Hearts?" swaggering along Princes Street, giggling in doorways, fighting in Rose Street. Their conduct proved that they had not seen the light, let alone the red light. Mansie was, of course, aware that a number of them regularly attended church on Sunday morning. But he had formed his own conclusions about that. The Presbyterians went to church because they were afraid of their fathers, the Roman Catholics went to church because they were afraid of the priest, and the Episcopalians because they were afraid they might miss an invitation to dinner. There were no flies on Mansie.

Brother Jeroboam's oratory held one unanswerable appeal. His view of the universe was consistent and presented the same face in all directions. That was why the communist speakers so hated Brother Jeroboam. Once their philosophy had been like his, a matter of pure theory with not a single human flaw in its logic. But now there were cracks, which questioners strove to widen with their inquisitive fingers. In the eyes of a youth in search of a complete and watertight philosophy, the Children of Gabriel occupied a very strong position.

Brother Jeroboam's system also possessed the pre-eminent virtue of simplicity. He taught that the Day of Judgment was at hand for the Cities of the Plain. The cities of the plain were Edinburgh and Glasgow, although he never put it so specifically, and there was a distinct understanding that places like Melrose and Pitlochry would escape more lightly, which seemed only fair as they had missed a good deal of the fun. The day was at hand because they had abandoned the Word of God, and, acknowledging kinship with monkeys, had come to resemble monkeys more than the creator in

26

whose image they were made. The day had not been appointed for an earlier date, because the present generation was living on the accumulated capital of its godly ancestors, but it was being rapidly moved forward and might be expected shortly.

In answer to a question as to how he could be so certain, Brother Jeroboam said, as calmly as if he had been asked how he knew that the nine-five to Glasgow was still running, that it was writ in the prophetic books, as in a time-table, and that it was the whole burden of the Book of Revelations. That silenced them. Asked what steps the Children would take in this emergency, he replied with confidence that the Children of Gabriel, under guidance, would be tipped off in advance and would immediately retire to the Pentland Hills, from which they could command a fine view of the destruction of the city. Further asked how he could be so sure of the visibility on that occasion, Brother Jeroboam smiled and ventured the observation that the Lord was not likely to put on a show on that scale and forget to allow his Children to see it. The atom bomb, wielded by all warring nations at one moment against one another, was to be the instrument of vengeance.

There was a completeness, a totality, in these retorts which caused a blissful satisfaction to expand through Mansie's brain. So often, when his mother was listening to these wireless services, he had overheard the most distinguished churchmen of the age confessing that now they saw as in a glass darkly. This struck him as scarcely good enough, indeed as a piece of impertinence. It was like driving through a fog, and being told to step on the accelerator by someone who did not know that there was a stone wall a couple of yards ahead. For Brother Jeroboam there was no fog. He saw as through a telescope on a clear sunny day.

When Mansie observed the riotous behaviour of the crowds on Princes Street and read of atom warfare in his evening paper, he felt that Brother Jeroboam's system was not only coherent but that it had probability on its side. But does one ever act upon intellectual conviction alone? Mansie might never have stepped off into Jordan, if he had not begun to envy the radiant happiness of the Children. It was borne in upon him that the Children were different. He had listened to divines who appealed to their flocks to face the world with courage. They were to be brave, with the high and hopeless heroism of the sailor on the sinking ship, to keep a stiff upper lip as they filed through a murderous world. But the Children were not afraid, because there seemed to be no reason for fear. In particular, Brother Jeroboam's smile was an instrument of infinite subtlety unlike the constant holy grin of Brother Methuselah or the consecrated glad eye of Sister Dinah. As he spoke of tumbling walls, blazing ruins and bomb-blasts like the snoring breath of an infuriated dragon, he tempered his apocalyptic vision by his smile. At that moment it became a rather sad smile, as if to say that the Children of Gabriel were aware of their preferential treatment, and had only one regret, that more of their fellow-citizens would not join them in their Pentland Hills grandstand. The smile suggested an inner beauty; which they did not want to boast of but could not quite conceal.

The smile it was that pulled it off. Brother Jeroboam had come to recognise Mansie's white, blank face in the audience, and he knew that sooner or later he must make the kill. Mansie as good as declared his thoughts by asking a question.

"What rule do the Children of Gabriel follow in their personal lives?"

Brother Jeroboam's smile was a masterpiece. For a moment he might have been a horse-faced Raphael bending over little Tobias. He made answer:

"We follow the rule of prayer, meditation and mutual sympathy. We share our burdens one with the other, and lay our sins together before the Lord, who takes them away."

So far so good, thought Mansie, at mention of this mystical dust collection, and begged leave to make one further enquiry. Leave was winningly granted.

"What attention, if any, is paid to the Ten Commandments?"

"We are far from disowning the Ten Commandments," replied Brother Jeroboam with a magnanimous smile, "but just as a citizen of Edinburgh does not constantly refer to the bye-laws of the burgh, so the Children of Gabriel are inclined to take the Ten Commandments as read. You see, my young friend, those who have been changed, naturally observe the Ten Commandments, even if they have never read them, but not all those who observe the Ten Commandments will stand there, in shining robes, on the last day."

This was an eminently satisfactory answer, for although he could not restrain a sneaking sympathy for those who had kept the rules but found themselves excluded from the final grand reception on a somewhat mysterious technicality, Mansie believed with Robert Burns,

> "The heart's aye the part aye,
> That makes us richt or wrang."

Brother Jeroboam judged that the critical moment had been reached. He struck promptly into his routine of prayer and appeal. In less than no time Mansie stood on the safe bank of Jordan, the ooze of sin and shame still trickling off his boots. He was wrung by the hand as the lighted tramcars jangled past, and the jarring sects raised their voices in controversy and the idle sightseers grinned and nudged each other in the ribs.

The Children were of Gabriel because Gabriel is the archangel who bears tidings, and their mission lay in bringing the tidings into the world. The Mound, like Hyde Park, is admirably suited for head-on collisions between the world and the truth, but after their missionary gesture had been made, the Children returned rejoicing to their headquarters, the Cave Adullam, a rented house in a part of the New Town which had become as shabby as Craigleith Stone would ever allow. Brother Methuselah at once retired to a dark closet to count the takings; Sister Dinah led a working party to brew tea; and Brother Jeroboam, in a conspicuously unobtrusive way, retired for a few minutes of private devotion to the Inner Sanctuary. This was a small chapel used only by such high priests.

The ordinary Children gathered in one of the larger rooms, which also declared itself to be a chapel of sorts. A wooden cross hung from the end wall, near which stood a table and lectern. On the walls there were set out prints of Biblical scenes. When Mansie found himself the silent new member among a chattering throng of Children, he did not notice these so clearly as the green floor-covering, which was extended up the wall for a distance of six feet. At that moment Brother Gamaliel, who was always given the heavy lifts, brought in a tray loaded with plain white cups.

"Excuse me, Brother," said Mansie, "can you please tell me why the linoleum goes up the walls?"

"'Tisn't linoleum," said Brother Gamaliel, "the best rubber, thirty-seven and nine a yard. We had to lay it because the influence kept draining away."

Brother Gamaliel hurried off to fetch a tea-urn. Still not absolutely clear on the subject, Mansie persisted in his enquiries and found a Child who said that after a service the room was full of healing influence. It had been seeping through the floor-boards into the basement, but the rubber had cured that.

"What about the door?" asked Mansie.

"I agree a certain amount of influence is lost every time the door is opened. If you notice, we slip in and out very quickly, but there can be no doubt it would be better if the door were sealed up and we descended by ladder through the ceiling from the room above. I expect that improvement will be made in time, though with the Day so close at hand, I doubt if it is worth the outlay."

31

Tea was friendly. Brother Methuselah smiled more than ever, and Brother Jeroboam seemed to take a delight in showing the newer members what a simple, happy soul he was.

"I was watching you, Brother, as you dallied on the brink. I think we shall call you Brother Naaman, for Naaman also tarried before he surrendered to the healing flood."

After tea there was a meeting, at which the new brothers and sisters were presented. Then the Children began to share their experiences of how they had overcome temptation. It had been a very tempting but triumphant week.

One sister confessed that she had been left alone in a back sitting-room with six ounces of Shetland wool belonging to a friend. She was an ounce short for the jumper she was knitting at the time and could easily have purloined one. Just as her fingers were poised, however, she realised that the Devil had arranged this curious and propitious conjunction of circumstances. She withdrew her itching fingers.

"Well fought, Sister!" exclaimed Brother Jeroboam, without much enthusiasm. "I suggest one Hallelujah."

"One Hallelujah," agreed Brother Methuselah.

The Children raised their voices in a half-hearted Hallelujah, while the sister looked crestfallen, having expected two.

That, however, was a mere beginning. Single Hallelujahs were awarded to a brother who conquered his vice of swearing although paint was spilled on his new suit, and to a sister who handed in her notice immediately upon being kissed in the nape of the neck by her employer. These were quite recent Children, the older hands realising that such paltry confessions could earn only the minimum of glory.

The first to score two Hallelujahs was a brother who had beaten his wife black and blue, and in the subsequent fit of remorse had implored her to beat him. She refused, on the ground that her own bruises would not become any less painful, whereupon he ran at the wall with his head and knocked himself senseless for fifty minutes. Another who had yielded to strong drink in a sensational degree and was expiating his offence by contributing round for round to the Glad Tidings Fund (he was one of those topers who take a morbid delight in recalling every financial detail next morning) was awarded a couple, although it might have been argued that he was purchasing them in hard cash.

Three Hallelujahs seemed to be reserved for victories over fleshly lust. You could have heard a pin drop as Sister Dinah described her adventure with a charming young plumber on whom she had taken pity as it was a cold day. She invited him to join her in a cup of tea. Not realising the innocent benevolence of her intention, he had mistaken the invitation for one of a different sort. In normal circumstances this might have been worth no more than two, but Sister Dinah so eloquently conveyed the amorous charm of the plumber, the crimped waviness of his hair and her own disturbed feelings, that it was unanimously agreed that she had been close indeed to the Devil's talons, and fully merited her three. As he listened, Mansie thought what a cold-blooded fish

33

he was by comparison, and despaired of ever winning similar applause.

Mansie's disillusion came as a consequence of the Day of Judgment, which indeed it was for the Children. At one meeting Brother Methuselah, who took the collection and said but little, suddenly stood up and announced that the Day of Judgment was to be next Friday. To the surprise of everyone no one was more sceptical than Brother Jeroboam. Yet he could not prevail, for the beatitude of Brother Methuselah's smile gave him unique authority. As Brother Methuselah's glowed with ever brighter wattage, Brother Jeroboam's evaporated from his ashen face, and he sought with frantic anxiety to undermine the credence of the little assembly.

It was an impossible task. For years he had been preaching the imminence of this day, and now the guidance was to hand, by a messenger so reliable as Brother Methuselah, who told in some detail his vision. The archangel, it seemed, had personally acquainted him with the date. Everyone realised that it was something of a slap in the face that Gabriel should have chosen Methuselah rather than Jeroboam. But, they told Jeroboam, such choices have always been unaccountably perverse. It was a recognition of the saintliness of their brother, which they had all noted, for Brother Methuselah never gave tongue, and was therefore no longer tempted as others were. In vain did Brother Jeroboam reason. For so long had he dealt in mystical certainties that the rational fell dreary and unconvincing from his lips. The Children loved an inspired and certain utterance. They were with Brother Methuselah to the last man and woman.

Friday had no doubt been chosen for the convenience of the Children, who met then in any event. It was resolved, despite the protests of Brother Jeroboam, that no one should go to work in the afternoon but that they should pack sandwiches and meet in St Andrew Square at 1.15p.m. Everyone was slightly hysterical. When Brother Jeroboam wanted to speak, someone called for a hymn, and they all set off for home, with shining faces.

Mansie's face was shining too, but he had not walked more than half-way home before the shine was gone. Although in theory it was pleasant to think of the world and certain individuals in it such as Ned Turpin, receiving its just deserts, he had preferred to think of this as occurring at some remote date, when he personally had finished with the world. He was walking along Heriot Row. Never had it seemed more solid. Worse than that! The Jupiter Assurance Mind could not encompass the chaos into which their nation-wide organisation would be tossed.

And what was he to do with Mother? That perplexed and worried him most of all. He could not leave her behind on such an occasion, yet he was convinced that nothing would persuade her to take a serious view of Brother Methuselah's prognostication. She would tell him it was time he grew up; she would dare him to endanger his coveted post.

Instead of breaking the news to her, he found himself remarking that it was a clear night but that a ring round the moon presaged somewhat more broken weather.

Then he slipped off to bed. A man who knows that the end of the world will come before the end of the week does not sleep well, but Mansie had known many a worse night's rest.

When Friday came, Mansie slipped round to St Andrew Square at the lunch hour. To his surprise there was a miserable turn-out. For one thing, Brothers Jeroboam and Methuselah were missing. So were Brother Gamaliel and Sister Dinah. Only a few men and women of one Hallelujah standing had put in an appearance. From the shelter of a shop door on the other side of the road he watched them confer beside the bus. One or two jumped on as the driver put it into gear, but the others drifted off home. Mansie returned to the office.

At three o'clock the afternoon became overcast. A superstitious shiver ran down Mansie's spine, and for a moment he wondered if he had been mistaken. But almost immediately a heavy shower of rain fell, making him thankful he was not out on the Pentlands. Then the sun burst forth. You could see right across the Forth. The sands of Aberdour were glinting, and the sight of the Lomond Hills filled him with genial relief.

His curiosity swelled during the remainder of the afternoon. As soon as the Jupiter closed, he made his way to the Cave Adullam. The door was ajar; he pushed it open and stole in. There was a mysterious sense of life in the house, but at first he saw no one. The large meeting-room was empty, though some cash notebooks lay in disorder on the table. He went upstairs, to the floor where Brother Jeroboam had his quarters. He heard a feminine voice laugh behind one of the doors and recognised it as Sister Dinah's. This is strange, thought Mansie, who had a guileless mind. Why should Sister Dinah be in Brother Jeroboam's quarters? The theory was beginning to suggest itself that Brother Jeroboam might be indisposed, when the door opened and Brother Gamaliel, stripped to the waist, walked on to the landing, carrying a tea-pot. He was all hair and muscle.

"Hello, Brother Naaman!" he exclaimed. "What are you doing here? Why aren't you on the Pentlands?"

"Why are you not there yourself?" asked Brother Naaman politely.

An impatient look appeared in Brother Gamaliel's eye.

"Mind your own b —," he began. But he subsided and added in a sulky voice, "I was detained. I was going out later."

At that moment Sister Dinah appeared in the door. Her hair was in disarray and she was wearing what appeared to be an old dressing-gown of Brother Jeroboam's. Her eyes were sparkling; there was a bloom on her cheek. Everything seemed uproariously funny.

"Don't blame Brother Gamaliel!" she laughed. "As for Sister Dinah, no more Hallelujahs for her! Don't want Hallelujahs! Much over-rated, Hallelujahs!"

"What are you two doing in Brother Jeroboam's room?" Mansie could not but enquire.

"We're having afternoon tea," said Sister Dinah, laughing so much that Brother Jeroboam's dressing-gown nearly fell apart. Mansie averted his eyes.

"I think I will go home," was all he could say.

"I should, if I were you," said Sister Dinah. "Hurry up, honeybunch!"

As he descended the stairs, supporting himself by the smooth mahogany banister, Mansie realised that the final remark was not addressed to him. How he had adored Sister Dinah! It was not quite plain till that instant.

Passing by the Inner Sanctuary he heard a snore. For a fleeting second he told himself that he had had enough, but the old obstinacy of the Thins arose in him. He turned the knob. The door opened. Inside was a small room, in the small room a large chair, and in the large chair Brother Jeroboam fast asleep, with his head back and his mouth open.

Mansie had never seen Brother Jeroboam asleep before. Ah, if we could first see our acquaintances asleep, how few of them we should ever cultivate! Wiped off was the smile of inner beauty, the eloquent mobility had congealed into cunning and greed, his teeth were like fangs and his gaping nostrils were shaggy with tufts of brown hair. A bottle of whisky, two-thirds empty, stood on a table and an empty glass had fallen over on the floor.

Mansie shook him.

"Brother Jeroboam! Brother Jeroboam!" he called. "Please tell me! What has happened?"

He repeated his questions as he gradually agitated the inert form into wakefulness.

"What has happened?" Brother Jeroboam at last replied. "I've been a sucker, my friend; that's what has happened! Have a drink!"

Mansie declined as Brother Jeroboam poured out another for himself.

"I've been a sucker! I might have known that rat Methuselah was out to double-cross me when he launched out on that spiel about the last day! My friend, your brother Methuselah has vanished, taking with him the Glad Tidings Fund!"

"Vanished, Brother Jeroboam?"

"Yes. Oh what a sucker I've been!" Brother Jeroboam groaned. "I trusted him. It was his smile. I ought to have known better!"

"What will happen to the Children?" Mansie asked.

The other paused for a moment, then spoke with sober ferocity.

"As far as I am concerned, the Children may go and take a running jump at themselves. My young friend, in case you should ever find yourself leading a revival of this nature, I give you one word of advice, out of the fruits of my experience. By all means prophesy the end of the world, but never name the day!"

Brother Jeroboam gazed at Mansie as at a disciple.

"You've everything to lose and nothing to gain by such a step. You mark my words, this deviation into exactitude has wrecked the Children of Gabriel, as well that unspeakable twister could foresee!"

"I will run along to the police," said Mansie, anxious to do the right thing.

"No, no, my young friend," cried Brother Jeroboam with surprising spirit and alacrity. "The police can do no good. I don't want the police! I shall depart for the other place. Edinburgh is worked out. If you will not object to my saying so, when I reached you, Brother Naaman, I was scraping up the dregs. But have a drink!"

Mansie declined and retired, apparently unnoticed by Brother Jeroboam. Just before he closed the front door, he heard a gentle screech from the floor above.

CHAPTER
FOUR

Cane-Conscious

How tempting it would be to write of the vacuum of disillusion in the soul of Magnus Thin! No one could deny that he felt a powerful sense of loss. One cannot be deluded in one's whole cosmogony and not notice the difference. But much more powerful than the emptiness of disbelief was the anger that he should have permitted himself thus to be had. Unwittingly to be the dupe — a painful, unnerving and irritant experience. But it must be undergone before a man may view other men and their pretensions with distrust.

"Oh, I wish the Day of Judgment had taken place!" Mansie cried as he walked through the evening air, oppressed by the sense of his own muggishness. Something caused him instantly to add, "Perhaps it is as well that it did not."

The small mingling with the great makes a farce of life. Mansie could not prevent himself from noting that whereas the weather forecast had promised easterly gales and a stream of gaseous frigidity direct from Siberia, the sun, in its customary preferential fashion, was bathing the West End in glory. Some peripheral beans were even striking upon the poorer parts of the city. Just as the rainbow promises no more floods of preposterous dimensions, the azure heavens appeared to whisper, "Cheer up. You'll rise above it."

As Mansie mulled over the vast mysteries to which he had just mislaid the key — never, he could not but feel, to find it again this side the grave — a smaller worry, unworthy of a free man and independent thinker, began to intrude. What explanation could he offer to his mother? He was now doubly relieved that he had not mentioned the event scheduled for that afternoon. That proves, he reflected, that I am not the dope Brother Jeroboam supposes me to be. Had I been that dope, I should at this moment be sitting on the Pentland Hills. The sandwiches would be finished, it would be turning rather chilly (what with the approach of eve and the lack of exercise) and the honest doubters would be raising their voices. No, I am not that much of a dope.

Recalling his varied emotions during the week that was past, he began even to muster up a little pride in his scepticism. Although unwilling to give himself credit, he had detected the distinctive aroma of fish. Still, that did not help to settle what he should say to his mamma.

Some male instinct of duplicity told him that it would be safer to preserve a diplomatic silence about the end of the world and to dwell instead upon the moral collapse of the Children. There might be an element of cowardice in such a course, but discretion was a more agreeable name for it. Mansie's experience was proving to resemble the electrical treatment by which modern physicians attempt to uncloud the addled mind. The cook, with the aid of egg-shells, clears the soup.

Mansie's egg-shells were the flimsy casings of his shattered convictions, and under their influence many obscurantist particles began to sink to the bottom.

Mrs Thin, who might have been caustic had he told the whole story, accepted with sagacious nods the account which rested upon the moral turpitude of the Children. There was no discredit in a well-brought-up innocent's failure to diagnose their inner baseness, although a woman of the world could tell that there must be something far wrong with a sect not permitted on the wireless.

Mansie began to feel as if some change were taking place in him. Once his mother caught sight of a smile flitting across his face. Usually, if Mansie smiled, there had to be some good reason, like one clown emptying a bucket of water down another clown's trousers at the circus, and this phenomenon disturbed her. It was something she could not fathom.

"What are you smiling at, Mansie?" she asked.

Mansie looked at her. He was thinking hard.

"It is only a slight touch of flatulence," he at length replied.

Dishonest, perhaps — but what can a young man do? One is not obliged to tell all one's thoughts, and a lie seemed kinder. Besides, how could she have understood that a cheerful voice was whispering to him, "Perhaps the old world *has* ended! Perhaps even now the new is setting, like a jelly cooling on a shelf. Wait a little longer, and you will be able to take a delicious bite!"

It was on the very next day that Mansie first became aware of walking-sticks and canes. He had long been familiar with the umbrella, for his mother possessed a fine specimen. This umbrella had a long, slender shaft, topped by a snipe-like bird's head and beak in ivory. It had such an old-fashioned look that if one had left it about, a museum would have grown up round it, but Mrs Thin guarded it as if it were her totem pole. In a sense you might have called it that, for she had received it at the hands of her Aunt Jeannie, a sister of her father's, long deceased. All Mrs Thin's family were long deceased, yet she venerated them in the umbrella. Whenever she dressed to pay a social call, she took the umbrella with her. It gave her as much sense of her own station as if it had been an ambulant family tree.

With the umbrella, then, Mansie was familiar, but he had never been conscious of walking-sticks. True, if you had handed him a walking-stick and asked him, in your best quiz-master's manner, to name the object, he would have replied, "A walking-stick." But the reason of the walking-stick, the underlying motive and theme-song, was a subject to which he had devoted no thought at all.

The Saturday after the world ended was a remarkably fine day. Mrs Thin had promised to sit in for the Chisholms so Mansie went for a walk in the Royal Botanic Garden and Arboretum. And there, sitting in the sun on a wooden bench, under a tree from Northern Manchuria, he first became cognisant of the walking-stick. This bench was his favourite. Sometimes, when he found it already occupied, he burned with crackling anger inside, hating the persons resting upon it and longing to topple them off a high cliff. But to-day it was vacant. Mansie preferred it because of a certain aloofness and privacy in its situation. All-seeing, you were not yourself stared upon.

The first man to pass was grey, corpulent and lame in one leg. Walking was such a task that facing it daily had worn a little furrow across his brow. He knew that if he misjudged the placing of his game leg, which was stiff at the knee and two inches shorter than the other, he would be unable to recover himself and would topple helplessly over, not only injuring himself but at the same time irreparably damaging the valuable plants from the Austrian Tyrol, Iceland and the Yukon. To him the stout ash walking-stick was a prop and a stay. He passed out of sight, leaving a series of little holes where the heel of his bad foot turned in the gravel.

It was strange that Mansie should have felt the first tiny stab of desire for a stick of his own at that moment.

"It is not as if I had a tucky leg," he told himself in reproof.

Just then he caught sight of a second man with a stick. This time the stick was white, so that Mansie knew the man to be blind. He could scarcely have told otherwise than by the colour, for there was no ominous Blind Pew tapping. The stick was poised above the grass margin, which every few yards it touched like an antenna, withdrawing slightly again. When the man reached a forking of the path, the antenna worked a little harder for a second or two, then off he moved with new certainty upon the chosen road.

"I am not blind," said Mansie peevishly. "I would look very silly with a stick."

You will observe that he did not speculate whether he had any need of a stick, merely on his appearance at the end of a stick. A stage was passed.

At that moment a third man swung into sight. He carried a shiny brown cane with which he cut lightly at the withered herbage of some exotic grasses. The cane whistled pleasantly in the air. Next he played a forehand drive, reminiscent of Cochet, quickly followed by a Tilden backhand return, in some mystical game of tennis, which continued until his racquet became a cricket bat. All too soon this man caught sight of one of the rangers in their blue uniforms and ex-service ribbons, and guiltily tucked the cane under his arm.

"He is neither blind nor lame," thought Mansie, "yet it suits him very well."

This opinion had barely hatched in his old incubator when he saw a fourth man, who also wielded a stick and who thought he had the Royal Botanic Garden and Arboretum to himself. He was conducting an orchestra of perhaps one hundred and fifty players through some mighty symphonic work. His beat was good and clear. He indicated each instrumental entry with clarity, eliciting the most subtle phrasing now from the beech trees, now from the azaleas, now from the rhododendrons. He secured a fine blending of tone in a chord sequence of herbaceous perennials, and evoked some oboe-like effects from the Japanese cherries. This fourth man caught sight of Mansie behind a flurry of lime leaves, blushed scarlet and let his baton fall weakly to his side just as he was approaching the climax of the first movement. The trees were mutely disordered and took some time to sort themselves out. The conductor hurried from sight.

And then came the fifth man, so young, so gallant, in flannel trousers, a sports jacket and a canary pullover knitted in cable stitch. He too thought the coast was clear, and handled his slim tiger's tail of a cane as if it were a rapier. With left hand raised above the shoulder and hand shaped like a ballet dancer's, he cut, thrust and parried. Only when with a deep lunge he had killed his man, did he convert his rapier into a sabre and battle at head level against overwhelming weight of numbers, as Richard Burton warded off the assegais of a hundred dervishes at the front door of his tent. So heavy was the engagement that the young man did not see Mansie at all. As he turned the corner out of sight, he straightened up and became commonplace again.

On his way home Mansie felt his hands idle and disengaged. All the emptiness of life seemed to have been transferred to the palm of his right hand.

Yet it was chiefly the encounter with Ned Turpin as he was returning up the stone staircase of No. 2 that drove Mansie to buy the malacca cane. On the second landing he heard the clip-clip of Myrtle's high heels on the flight above. Immediately her small feet and ankles of surpassing beauty appeared at the turn of the stair. Modestly averting his eyes, Mansie stepped aside to allow her to pass.

Had she been slightly older or slightly younger, Myrtle would have been content to smile, to comment upon the state of the weather and to descend with expedition to the street. But she had arrived at the precise age when no man is too unpromising to be ignored. Beneath the most phlegmatic exterior there may lurk the source of some excitement. She had also, with the sure instinct of the female, discerned the disapproval of Mrs Thin. Mrs Thin, she felt certain, regarded her as a forward young madam. Without having recourse to the process of reason, she perceived that if she could appear favourably in Mansie's eyes, she might start a train of internal dissension and cause Mrs Thin much subtle and indirect annoyance.

She opened her eyes wide and brought the dimmers up to full. Mansie felt both alarmed and exhilarated, as if he had suddenly been left naked in the middle of a sunlit beach. Before he could recover himself, she breathed in a shy, soft, friendly voice, "Hello, Mansie." He gained a distinct impression that in some way he overawed her. Common sense ought to have pointed out to him that this was fallacious, but the beam from her eyes had frizzled his common sense as if it had been made of inferior celluloid.

"Hello, Myrtle," he replied, unable to keep the tremor out of his voice.

"I was just saying to myself to-day, what has happened to Mansie," she went on, pausing opposite him and no more than a foot away, so that he shrank against the wall. "I don't seem to have run into you for donkey's years."

Mansie could not but appreciate that there was something rather stylish, arch and fashionable in her use of the phrase "for donkey's years." He was a little stunned to learn that she was evidently keeping a secret tally of his public appearances. He had never thought that any store was set upon his comings and goings, except by his mother, whose interest could be partly explained by the technicalities of household administration. No one could allege that Myrtle's interest depended on such points as when to put a light under the frying-pan.

He replied, "Oh, I'm always about."

"I sometimes see you up on Princes Street on Sunday night," she pursued. "Oh, but I forgot! You don't approve of us girls walking the carpet on Princes Street! I wouldn't miss it for a million dollars! Anyway, what can you see in these types havering at the Mound? I think they're queer!"

She clearly did not know of his infatuation for the Children of Gabriel. He was relieved.

"I wouldn't call them queer," he said defensively. "They put forward very unusual and interesting theories."

"Well, they can keep them for me!" said Myrtle lightly.

This was the point at which the iron-shod shoes of Ned Turpin were heard clattering down from the third landing. The last person capable of behaving in a civilised way was Ned Turpin. By nature he could not let slide any single chance to throw his weight about and to make unpleasantness.

"Just look!" he exclaimed, halting on the step above the landing so that with his natural advantage in height he towered some eighteen inches above Mansie. "Will you get a load of that! See who our Myrtle's having a *tête-à-tête* with! Skinny in person! Come along, my girl, you're wasting your time! You won't get very far with young fish-face!"

"Ned Turpin!" Myrtle exclaimed in protest — rather feeble protest, Mansie thought.

He felt that now was the time to assert his manhood by some devastating speech or action, but he could think of nothing to say, and when he tried to say it he choked. "If only I had a stick!" he found himself wishing. Ned Turpin was not so tongue-tied.

"Come on, hen!" he said, seizing Myrtle by the arm in an offensively casual way which she appeared not to resent. "I'll cheer you up! I'll chum you as far as the tram."

With that he swept her off downstairs, pushing Mansie against the wall by the merest touch of a shoulder charge as he passed. Although he knew that Ned was going with her no farther than the tram-stop, his sensations might be compared with those of a gentleman Sabine who happened to be about during the Rape of the Sabine Women. He was smarting under the twin indignities of being pushed and of having his *tête-à-tête*, broken up. Not that he had sought the *tête-à-tête*, not that he judged Myrtle to be other than a very frivolous young woman — but all the same his ears went scarlet, his eyeballs throbbed, and he longed for a stick, a loaded stick for preference, with which to beat Ned Turpin insensible, by way of a sharp lesson.

This was how Mansie came to feel that he had need of a cane. With a cane in his paw, he would not be quite so defenceless in this labyrinthine, deceitful and hostile world.

As for Myrtle, such adventures made her day.

CHAPTER
FIVE

The Malacca Cane

There are so many second-hand shops in Edinburgh that the wants of the inhabitants might be supplied from them alone, and were it not for an ineradicable love of novelty in the hearts of the inhabitants, the numerous splendid modern emporia would be left without a function. What man of sound judgment would buy a new armchair when old chairs are always so much more comfortable? Indeed, it is an axiom that chairs cannot achieve comfort till they are old. Think of anything necessary to human life — shoe-trees, snuff mulls, flint-lock pistols, strips of Oriental silk, fireproof earthenware dishes. One can find all these objects and many more in the second-hand shops, and not in the brashness of their original state either, but mellowed by handling and use. As men of ripe character and experience cannot but overshadow untried youths, so they outshine the products of this age with a quiet superiority which does not depend on the arts of window dressing.

The second-hand shops of Edinburgh fall into three categories — those which sell to the Americans, those which have some expectation of making a sale to a native, and those to which a customer comes as a rare and barely credible surprise, and is reported like a new comet. In shops of the first class, they tell you the price of their silver in a contemptuous way, having recognised by your clothes and your accent that you cannot afford it. In those of the second, as they name the price they watch you narrowly, and instantly reduce it if they read inability to pay in your eyes. In the third category, the shop is rarely open, or if it should chance to be open, then no one is to be found in charge of it. There appears to be nothing to prevent a casual stranger from walking off with the entire stock-in-trade. Such notices as "Gone away. Back at three," or "Enquire at No. 77." are constantly to be read, in joiner's pencil on the reverse of grubby envelopes in the shop window. Yet here it is, if one has the patience, that the bargains are to be found. Here one may pick up, for a shilling, a table with one leg missing, a chest of drawers infested with wood-worm, pillows from which the feathers fly on every breeze, cameras as large as concertinas (the lens cracked and the shutter out of order), venerable typewriters the letters of which are fixed on a drum that has ceased to revolve. Here, too, come to rest all the umbrellas, walking-sticks and canes of the dead.

Mansie was paid on Fridays. Ever since he began to work, he had placed, under his mother's tutelage, such a sum as he could afford in the Post Office Savings Bank. The remainder he handed to his mother, keeping back ten shillings to be his week's pocket money. Of those ten shillings, as many as six had been finding their way every week into the coffers of the Children of Gabriel. Even at this moment, thought Mansie, my shillings are supporting Brother Methuselah in some comfort. The reflection in no way consoled him.

As soon as the Friday following the disintegration of the Children of Gabriel the self-denying Mansie was conscious instead of the itch of extravagance. He wanted to spend some money. The ten shillings — in particular, the six that would have been ear-marked for the Glad Tidings Find — were burning a hole in his pocket.

During the week Mansie had pondered much upon walking-sticks and had as good as admitted to himself that he intended to buy one. Being unversed in the ways of the world, his first thought was to buy a stick in one of the new emporia. In multiple stores he was bold and confident, for in the ironmongery department it is always possible to say that what you really want is a pair of tennis shoes and thus escape if the price is beyond your means, but these shops that sell only one article present a ticklish problem. One can scarcely enter a walking-stick shop and then, after inspecting the stock, declare that one is looking for a safety razor. For a multitude of eager assistants swoop down before one's reconnaissance is complete.

There was, however, on Mansie's route to the Jupiter a renowned stick and umbrella shop. The first time he passed the window, he glanced coyly at the sticks from the corner of his eye but left them in some doubt if he were interested or not. The second time he paused and gazed at them with the same dispassionate curiosity that might be aroused by a herd of cows. I am interested in the spectacle he seemed to say, but nothing more. Then he looked for the price labels, but it was not that kind of shop. They would tell you inside or not at all. True, each stick or cane had a tiny circle of paper gummed to it. He was able to read the writing on one. "e/fl/p," it said. Code.

There was no other way than to enter. Mansie thought for twenty-four hours and did so. An assistant was hiding behind the door and pounced. With every wrinkle of his nose he said, "You are not the type of man who carries a cane."

But Mansie was ready for him.

"I have been delegated," he said, "by a small committee to enquire the price of a walking-stick which we intend to present to one of our colleagues as a token of our esteem and regard."

The assistant stroked his chin. A small committee? How small? If it were ten, at ten bob each, that meant he could sell a stick costing five pounds. The customer looked as if he could just rise to ten bob.

"I think we have just the article you are looking for," he replied, adding "sir" with palpable effort. "This ebony cane is eminently suited for presentations. The silver clasp is sufficiently large to permit of an inscription of suitable warmth."

"It is rather black," said Mansie critically, holding it up to the light.

"In ebony, sir, that is almost unavoidable," said the assistant. "If you will try the balance, you will find it excellent."

"Umm," said Mansie as he swung the cane, almost cracking the plate-glass counter in his clumsiness. "Sorry. How much did you say it was?"

"The price is —. Will you excuse me, sir?" The assistant took the cane, making a *moue* which suggested that the customers of that particular shop chose what they liked because they liked it, and asked about prices afterwards. "The price appears to be five pounds seventeen and three."

Mansie's face fell.

"Yes," said the assistant, "a remarkably cheap cane. The fact is, you are lucky. Pre-war stock. Better quality. Lower price. Our last, too. New canes of the same quality run a couple of pounds dearer. Not of course that you *can* get the same quality. Or ever will in my lifetime or yours. The political situation in the East."

"Thank you," said Mansie. "I think my proper course is to report back to the committee."

The assistant had no answer to that gambit. As he saw Mansie retreating to the door, he acknowledged that he had been too brusque.

"We shall esteem it a favour to be entrusted with your commission," he said. "A very mild afternoon, sir."

"So it would appear," retorted Mansie, "but there will be five degrees of frost in the night, probably towards morning."

There he had turned the tables on the assistant. He emerged on to the pavement without apparent loss of face. But his brow was moist. "No cane for me," he sighed regretfully. "No cane for Mansie Thin. Mansie Thin must continue to walk abroad naked and defenceless."

That evening his mother sent him out for a fish and chip supper. Mrs Thin, on the whole, disapproved of such expedients, which are the mark of the lower classes, but in spite of everything, she could not conceal a partiality for this old-world Scottish delicacy. It was not as if she or Mansie ever ate them on the street, out of the newspaper. They would sooner have been tortured at the stake. A wide gulf is fixed between those who devour them alfresco and wipe their greasy fingers on the seat of their pants, and those who convey them noiselessly home. Eating chips, like doing good, should be carried out by stealth. This Mrs Thin fully understood. Besides, there was a genteel little shop she knew of. The chips were cooked by a secret process, and were thus of superior succulence. The proprietor was an Italian gentleman of the old school, with the manners of a duke. There were no pin-tables or nickelodeons in his shop, and he never called his lady customers "hen." So Mansie was dispatched on this crucial evening of his life to buy chips.

The chip shop was situated in the Street of One Thousand Bargains, where most of the second-hand shops of the third category are to be found. It was quite dark, the street not being one of those favoured by the new diffused lighting, yet, as Mansie walked the length of it, a score of shining windows endued the neighbourhood with an air of underground gaiety, as if some resistance movement were celebrating independence day and had not been careful enough about the shutters. Absent from the windows of the second-hand shops were the "Gone away" and "Enquire" signs; shops which only a few hours earlier looked as if the owner had recently died now presented a front of some animation. Inside, by the light of a gas jet or a dusty unshaded electric bulb, Mansie could see the proprietors reading the evening paper.

One shop in particular arrested his attention by its varied display. In a vast pile, just inside the window, lay enough second-hand shoes, both ladies' and gents', to protect the feet of half the ladies and gents in the city. Mansie could not help wondering why people were always complaining about having to break in new shoes when here was such a wide selection already broken in. One could read the histories of the first wearers — their bunions, their struggle with French heels just half an inch too high, their assiduity in the art of dancing, their habit of braking their bicycles by applying the sole of the right foot to the surface of the front tyre. There were patent leather-boots which had been worn by eminent citizens, now deceased, at Merchant Company dinners, riding boots, and the distinctive footgear of former commanders in the Royal Navy. The relics of dandyism were declared in the elastic-sided boots, the slender pumps, the ornately punched brogues with thong laces, the strapped shoes with silver buckles. Round this pyramid, completely filling the shop window, there was much else to take the eye — a tennis racquet minus two strings, a dirty golf umbrella, a trout rod which had snapped under the weight of some enormous fish, or perhaps only when the hook caught on water-weed, a basin and ewer from a Victorian bedroom, the death mask of a sickly youth, companion pictures of Windsor Castle and Balmoral Castle, a claymore which had belonged to an officer in the Seaforth Highlanders, two China dogs, a bed-pan and a brown jar marked "rice."

At this point the walking-sticks caught Mansie's eye. A thick bundle of them, tightly bound together with old rope and looking like the lictor's faeces in ancient Rome, was lying, little regarded, at the back. The spectacle gave him fresh heart. Only then did he know how the thought that he must toil through life unassisted by a prop of any kind had distressed him. But now, perhaps. He almost entered the shop on the spur of the moment, but it was foreign to Mansie's nature to yield to such a precipitate urge. He controlled his impulse. With single-mindedness he set his face towards the chip shop.

But next evening found him back in front of the second-hand shop window. He would have liked a glimpse of the proprietor. One enters any situation with a little more confidence by being prepared. Unfortunately the window was so crammed with interesting objects that the inner shop was screened, and the glass panel in the door, through which he might have peered, was entirely filled by an engraving, of rare historical interest, depicting the Relief of Ladysmith. He pushed the door open with infinite caution, but the diabolically cunning shopkeeper had fixed a bell to it. A loud "ping" told him that, unless he cared to lose face, he must advance. He did.

As he peered about him, he could see that there was little room in which to manoeuvre, owing to the plentiful stock. He nearly struck his head on a hanging flower-pot, and beyond that he could see a chandelier. Indeed all the upper breathing space appeared to be filled with dependent objects. The ceiling was as full of mystery as the dim-lit vault of a crypt. All round him grew a forest of what-nots, hall-stands and tall-boys rising like stalagmites to meet the stalactites from the roof. An undergrowth of kitchen chairs, golf clubs and nursery fireguards further impeded his progress. A path, however, wound through it, leading to the back of the shop. Mansie followed the path, and soon emerged on to a clearing.

In the middle of the clearing sat an old woman wearing a working man's bonnet. As she looked up from the evening paper, Mansie noted that she had the beginnings of a beard. He was a little nervous of all women, but bearded women, with whom he had never before had dealings, terrified him. Bearded women must always appear formidable to beardless men, but inside they are full of regrets. She eyed Mansie sadly, but did not speak at first.

"I don't know if I want anything —," Mansie began.

Her gloom increased.

"If you don't know, son," she said, "you can be sure nobody else does."

"What I mean is, I don't know if I'm buying until I see whether you have what I want."

"Fair enough," admitted the bearded lady. "Nobody could take one iota of exception to that. And what might you be seeking, son?"

Although bridling a little at the "son," Mansie could do little but swallow it.

"Have you any walking-sticks?" he asked.

"Walking-sticks?" she repeated, and again, "Walking sticks? I think I have on these premises every walking-slick that ever rang on the plainstanes of Edinburgh. Were you wanting a stick for yourself, son?"

She spoke as one might to a child.

"I should like to examine a selection," replied Mansie with adult dignity.

"Son, seeing it's you, you can examine the whole perishing lot."

The bearded lady removed her buttocks from the chair and clove a path through a sea of kitchen utensils, till she reached the bundle of sticks.

"See, take your pick!" she exclaimed, with a reckless air. "You'll not see walking-sticks like them nowadays!"

She unfastened the ropes, so that the sticks rattled loose on the floor.

"Take all night to it!" said the bearded lady, and returned to the evening paper, in which she was studying the small ads. of articles wanted and for sale with narrow concentration.

Some of the sticks Mansie would not have been seen dead with. There was a blackthorn, for instance, so prickly and so knobbly that it might have been carried on to the stage of the "Empire" by the late Sir Harry Lauder, and earned a good laugh by itself. There were several which had maintained a respectable appearance in their upper halves, but having lost the ferrule, had worn down in the most distressing fashion, just like a man whose poverty is revealed by his boots. The heads of others were slack and wobbled at the touch.

A few could not be so lightly discarded. Mansie picked out one of these from the ruck. It had a straight ivory handle and a chased silver band, disgustingly tarnished.

"It will clean," said the bearded lady, without glancing up from her paper.

Mansie held the inscription up to the light.

"To Richard Mellodew," it read, "in memory of the old days, from a few of the boys."

For a moment, Mansie forgot his own urgent needs. Who was Richard Mellodew? Were "the boys" males below the years of maturity, or, as he suspected, some way above, and taking full advantage? He had a vision of boon companions rollicking home, arm in arm, after midnight. "The old days!" What an infinity of regrets was contained in these three words! They had lived too long, they were under doctor's orders and had to be in bed by ten. But one treasure no one could rend from them, the memory of the old days.

As if to confirm these deductions, the bearded lady looked up.

"Didn't that belong to the late Mr Mellodew?" she asked, taking the stick from his hand and peering at the lettering. "Aye, so it did. You would remember Mr Mellodew?"

Mansie confessed that he did not.

"Och, surely you must have seen him, late at night, on the way home from the bowling club. He fairly took the width of the road. To see him you would never have known that he played for the Hibernians in his prime. But that would be before your day."

"I don't think I could carry a stick marked 'Richard Mellodew'," Mansie began hesitantly.

"No, I don't think you could," agreed the bearded lady, with an emphasis on the "you" which did not appeal to Mansie. She returned to her evening paper.

He looked at several of the other sticks. One was inscribed, "To R.S.M. Watt, from Old Pals, the Sergeants' Mess, and Battalion, The Gordon Highlanders." Laconic, yet what a wealth of meaning was there contained. "To J. ('Jock') Neil," said another, "in memory of his triumphs with the small bore rifle. He was the king among us a'."

There was a masculine note about these inscriptions, like a blast on the trombone. Mansie studied one or two others. None of them seemed to be the expression of the sentiments of Women's Rural Institutes. The thought had just struck him, when his eye lit upon a cane, and as soon as it lit, he knew that it must be his. It had lain concealed under a pile of plebeian ash plants, otherwise it must have claimed his attention before. Even amid the dust of the junk shop, its silken, nutty gloss, red as one of those russet pebbles rubbed bright by the wet sea, shone out like a countess at a tenants' ball. It was tipped with an iron ferrule and surmounted by a silver ball, which fitted exactly into the palm of Mansie's hand. Made for him, as the saying is! It was weighty, yet slim, a cane of style and substance.

"Real malacca," said the bearded lady. "You don't see the likes of that nowadays."

"Is there a name?" asked Mansie, rotating the knob before his eyes.

"No, but you can see the hallmark. At least you could, if it was clean and we had a wee pickle more light on the subject," the bearded lady added truthfully.

Mansie could not help speculating.

"Whom did it belong to?" he enquired.

"Now who did Billy say? I wonder, did Billy ever tell me?" the bearded lady asked of a commode in the far corner. Then turning round upon her customer, "I declare I don't believe he ever mentioned it," she said. "Billy picked that up, not me. I'm sorry, son, I can't tell you."

"Could we ask Billy?" Mansie suggested.

"No, we couldn't," the bearded lady answered with great firmness. "He went and died on me last week."

This remark was followed by some moments of silence, partly out of respect to the late Billy, partly from the difficulty in finding the correct conversational progression. Mansie devoted himself more closely to a study of the cane, and yielded to the temptation of wiping off the dust on the lining of his overcoat. He felt the knob again on the palm of his hand. Even in this brief caress the black grease began to rub off on his skin and the silver gleamed winningly at him. Then, to his amazement, it twirled itself round, just striking an ornament of crystal drops which hung from the roof, and almost breaking it. The crystal drops tinkled in indigation.

"Canny, son!" cried the bearded lady. "Keep the malacca cane under control!"

She spoke exactly as if it were a mettlesome horse.

There now seemed no way of putting off asking the price.

"I'll give it you!" said the bearded lady at once. "Seven and six."

That anything so gorgeous should cost so little amazed Mansie. The bearded lady misread his expression. Quick as a flash she corrected herself.

"Seeing it's you, son, five bob!"

Mansie took two half-crowns from his trouser pocket, and handed them to the bearded lady, who accepted them without demur, as well she might, seeing she had cleared a profit of eight hundred per cent. For it is a melancholy fact that upon his decease a man can raise next to nothing on his old walking-stick, however sumptuous it may be.

Out in the street the malacca cane went berserk. It twirled round and round, revelling in its newly found freedom, and almost poked a pedestrian in the eye. Mansie had some trouble in curbing it, but by the time he reached No. 2 Bleachfield it was well in hand, only tugging slightly.

He went upstairs with new confidence, but at the door stopped short. He flinched from telling his mother. She was sure to ask what *he* wanted with a stick. So he placed it in the deep Chinese jar alongside Aunt Jeannie's umbrella. He did not say a word. But then, even when he was converted, he did not say a word.

They were sitting together before the kitchen fire when Mrs Thin, who never allowed her hands to lie idle, went off to look for some darning. Her errand took her through the tiny hall of the flat. Mansie had almost forgotten the malacca cane. Suddenly he heard a scream, followed by a a dull thud, which could only have been caused by the body of Mrs Thin falling to the floor.

"Good heavens," thought Mansie, "either we have a criminal concealed in the flat and he has socked her, or the rug has slipped on the polished floor, as it has done already."

Grasping the poker, he ran to her rescue. She was on the floor right enough, but no one else was to be seen. The door was latched and no one was hiding behind the coats. He knelt by her side. As he raised her head in the crook of his arm, she began to regain her senses.

"Mansie! Mansie!" she whispered.

"Yes, Mother? What happened?"

"Where did that cane come from?"

Mansie was puzzled.

"That cane? — I just bought it — this very evening."

"You didn't! Someone gave it to you!"

"Mother, I tell you I bought it. I paid five shillings for it. It's real malacca."

Mrs Thin was by this time sitting up and gazing at the stick as if it were a cobra about to dart at her.

"Take it away! It's . . . no, it can't be! It's not possible that it should be!"

Mansie was quite bewildered. "It's not possible that it should be what?" he asked.

Mrs Thin rose, withdrew her hand from his arm, and felt her way unsteadily to the kitchen.

"It doesn't matter," she said. "It's nothing."

Mansie was following her, in something of a twitter.

"But, Mother, it must be something! It made you faint!"

Mrs Thin was most indignant.

"What nonsense!" she exclaimed. "It did nothing of the kind. I was overcome by a sudden fit of giddiness. I think I must have indulged too heavily in the chips last night. For goodness sake, shut the door!"

CHAPTER
SIX

The Cane Begins to Tug

From that day Mrs Thin was a changed woman. By Mansie she was puzzled, by the cane overawed. In the morning, when she went out to work, she circled the malacca cane at a distance of two and a half feet, as one might skirt the leopard's cage at paw's reach. Yet her reticence on the subject was total. Although Mansie was puzzled, he could not penetrate it at any point, for while consumed with curiosity she refused to ask questions, beyond confirming on half a dozen occasions that he had purchased it and not received it as a gift. It seemed of vast importance to her that the cane should have reached him by a completely anonymous method.

Mansie also felt her intense dislike of the cane. Hatred — that was not too strong a word! He could see it in her eye as she passed through the hall. Sometimes he fancied that admiration was mingled with the hatred. In short, his mother's feelings about the cane appeared to be so complex that he gave up trying to unravel them. He lumped them together in the category of disapproval, and while to one who had basked so much in the sun of approval, the change was icy and unwelcome, it also stirred his obstinacy. He became more attached than ever to the malacca cane, and vowed that he would not willingly allow himself to be deprived of it. He never left the house without it. At night he laid it against the wall in his bedroom.

The cane had undoubtedly infected Mansie with an attack of wanderlust. He had always taken the tramcar from Bleachfield up to the Jupiter Assurance, but now he frequently walked. He always walked down the hill, even if he took the tram up, and it was remarked that he was learning to manage the stick like a gentleman. The fancyfree twirl, the sudden slash, the manner of placing the tip on the pavement, so that grace not support was evidently the object — all these evolutions, one by one, he mastered.

But let it not be thought that he mastered the cane. Say rather that the cane was beginning to master him. He would be sitting before the fire of an evening during that slack-water of the week — say Tuesday, Wednesday or Thursday. In the old days he would have been content to sit, worrying because Mr Woodburn had looked black at the office and gradually drowsing off into a sleep from which he awoke with a putrid taste in his mouth. Now his thoughts turned to the cane. It seemed to be calling him in a low tone from the hall, *sotto voce* so that his mother might not hear, but insistently, taunting him with the agreeable sting of the night air, the gaudy spectacle of the neon lighting in Leith Walk, the tramcars like mobile palaces a-glitter with a grand ball as they crossed the North Bridge. The first night that he heard it he resisted the lure, for his mother would think it odd if he were to go sailing through the painted darkness, but the second night the siren song was too sweet and clear to be ignored. He kicked off his slippers and began to lace up his shoes. As he did so, he remarked to his mother,

"I find the atmosphere somewhat oppressive in here to-night. I think I would be none the worse of a breath of fresh air. Besides, I am curious to know whether there is yet any sign of the heavy cloud drifting from the west which we were promised earlier this evening in the weather forecast."

Mrs Thin, who might have suggested opening the window by an inch or two, was caught off her guard by the meteorological argument. Before she had thought of a reply Mansie was in the hall, donning his overcoat, muffler and the cloth cap which he wore on more informal occasions. She could hear the rattle as he drew the malacca cane out of the china jar. She knew she was defeated, and had to content herself with calling out, rather piteously, "Don't be late home, Mansie!"

How many mothers have called those words after their sons, and always on the occasions when that is precisely what they are going to be!

Mansie had not reached the foot of the stair when he heard behind him a noise like Cinderella running. Looking back, he saw first of all golden dance slippers, then the hem of a Nile green dress, than a cherry-coloured overcoat and finally, on top of that, Myrtle.

"Hello, Mansie," she said, with unaffected surprise. "Fancy you out so late!"

"You have taken the very words out of my mouth," replied Mansie, with tender severity.

Myrtle giggled. Her eyes sparkled in a way that helped Mansie to feel he would recognise champagne.

"Just because you go to bed at nine," she replied, "do you suppose everyone else does?"

Mansie was at a loss for the right retort, but simply by smiling and twirling his cane neatly in the confined space, he somehow got the better of the argument.

"My goodness gracious me!" said Myrtle, when she saw the cane. She was almost as deeply impressed as his mother, though the strange sense of recognition was absent. "Where did you get a hold of that?"

"See — real malacca!" said Mansie proudly, half surrendering it for her inspection.

"My word!" she repeated. "Isn't that great?"

Before he knew, Mansie found himself opening the street door for Myrtle. He followed her on to the pavement, she half-turning to wait for him. "I cannot deny that I have a soft spot for Myrtle Bremner," he reflected. "Her head is empty but it is very graceful, and I perceive a musical quality in her laughter. Brains, at any rate, are over-esteemed and give far less pleasure than beauty."

Aloud he asked, with something of his old censoriousness, "Where are you off to at this time of night?"

"Where are you off to yourself?" she pertly retorted.

"I am in search of a breath of fresh air, purely and simply," he answered, with a slight emphasis on the "purely and simply," and continued with a glance at her dress, "but you are on your way to a do of some kind."

"If I am," said Myrtle, "that is entirely my own concern."

"I was not suggesting that it was not," Mansie acknowledged.

They walked a few paces towards the tram-stop, when Mansie made the discovery that women do not appreciate lack of curiosity.

"If you want to know," said Myrtle, "I have been handed a special invite to the Osiris."

"The Osiris?" repeated Mansie blankly. "What's that?"

In other walks of life nothing could exceed the annoyance of letting drop that one has been invited to the Savoy Grill and then discovering that as far as the audience is concerned it might be a good pull-up for night lorry-drivers. Myrtle pursed her lips.

"I should think you are the only person in this town who has never heard of it," she said.

"Perhaps that is so," admitted Mansie. Myrtle was afraid he might drop the subject, but the cane waggled and he added, "But all the same, may I ask what it is?"

"The Osiris is a dance club. Now don't tell me you've never heard of a dance club?"

"Yes, I have," said Mansie, "though never much good."

Myrtle flushed.

"Allow me to tell you, Mansie Thin," she retorted, "the Osiris is very select, high-class and chick."

"How did *you* get an invite?" he asked.

It was a natural question, and asked without the wish to offend, but if Mansie had been older or by nature more diplomatic, he would not have put it that way. Myrtle would have slapped his face, but she bit her lip instead. Such insinuations have to be answered.

"If you want to know, Madame Désirée gave it to me. She's one of our customers up at the shop. She's the hostess at the Osiris. Oddly enough, she thinks I'm a nice girl. Oddly enough, they only want nice girls at the Osiris."

"Why do they want girls at all?" asked Mansie.

"You are a big stupid, Mansie Thin!" Myrtle spat, red with annoyance. "I think Ned Turpin's right! You're a penny short in your change! How can you have dancing if you haven't girls?"

"I say!" Mansie opened his eyes in horror. "You're not going to be a dancing girl?"

Myrtle stamped her foot. "You make me tired! You really are obtuse! Can't you see? There must be partners for the men!"

"I thought that in all nice clubs the men brought their own partners."

"You don't expect them to carry their partners on a battleship, do you? There's an American cruiser in the Forth!"

Myrtle could have bitten out her tongue.

"It's news to me that American sailors are interested in nice girls," Mansie observed.

"Those are to be officers!" cried Myrtle, from the heart.

"It is still news!" retorted Mansie, twirling his cane.

"What do you think I am?" demanded Myrtle, facing him squarely and causing an obstruction on the pavement.

"Allow me to tell you I am not that kind of a girl. I was well brought up, and I can take care of myself. Your trouble is that you have a dirty mind."

"I'm glad to hear it," said Mansie. "I thought you implied I had no mind at all. I suppose even a dirty mind is better than a complete blank. Where is this Osiris? I have a very good mind to come and escort you home."

Myrtle glared at him like a pretty little wild-cat at the kitten stage.

"Just you dare, Mansie Thin!" she cried. "Just you dare, and I'll never speak to you again! In fact, I'll never speak to you again in any case!"

Turning swiftly from him, she leapt on to the No. 98 tram as it slowed down at the points. That is one way of ending an argument.

Mansie was left stranded, high and dry, on the pavement, but just as he began to feel cast-off and lonely, the cane described a congratulatory twirl. After all, he had displayed a certain authority, and ousted Myrtle in argument. He set off at a sprightly pace towards town. As he climbed the hill, the Victorian tenements gave way to the disdainful order of the Georgian terraces. A lovely night, but an American cruiser lay at anchor in the Forth and he was worried about Myrtle.

He was strolling along one of the more fashionable streets of the city, wondering what lay behind the muslin curtains when the malacca cane gave a sudden but unmistakable tug. Those who have practised the water-diviner's art know well the sensation. The inanimate twig lives in the hand and presses upwards. As well as pressing upwards, Mansie's cane pointed to the right, directly towards a door marked "The Gentleman's Lounge." Mansie recognised it as a bar of the more genteel sort.

Mansie held no truck with bars. There was one not very far from Bleachfield. Although he had never been inside, he smelt the disgusting odour of stale beer every time he passed the door and, on Saturday night, heard the raucous and displeasing voices of the customers as they sang "We're coming round the mountain." He had three principal objections to their musical exercises. Their songs were few, tuneless and audible. He had no desire whatever to enter the portals of the Bleachfield Bar. The Thins had never mingled with the *canaille*. Besides, Ned Turpin worked in a bar.

Yet he entered "The Gentleman's Lounge." True, there was no smell of stale beer or sound of singing. He entered simply because the cane led him so persuasively and firmly. And he stood there blinking, for his eyes had never beheld such a chamber of luminosity. Even the boardroom of the Jupiter Assurance with the new fluorescent lighting full on was nothing to it, The counter and the tables were of glass, from which beams shone as if the sun were a prisoner below in the vaults. There were mirrors and baubles everywhere, so that Mansie could watch himself receding into a distant wonderland. The bar was quiet, the citizens being very short of money at the time, yet the red-faced barman in the spotless dentist's jacket was grinning. He seemed such a healthy man.

Although inexpert in the ritual of bars, Mansie felt that he would be called upon to buy something, and that with promptitude and decision. Instinct told him that it would be no use pretending to wait till a friend came. In that he was right, for no mark so gives away the tyro in debauchery as a reluctance to come to grips with the grape or grain. The true initiates hold fast to the convention that wild horses will not separate them from the bottle and that waiting for a fellow-toper is an opportunity, not to be neglected, for snatching a flying start. Mansie was trying hard to remember the names of any drinks but could only remember whisky, the taste of which alone, when taken to cure toothache, was too much for him. It seemed that his ignorance could not be concealed when the healthy barman, who had been growing steadily more rubicund, exclaimed,

"Hello, hello, hello! My old friend, I never thought to see you again!"

Mansie stared at him in some alarm. If the cane had not stood fast, he would have turned tail and fled. He could have sworn that he had never clapped eyes on the healthy barman before that instant. And now the barman was extending his hand across the luminous counter, on which lay dishes of toasted potato shavings and of pearly onions. Under the compulsion of courtesy, Mansie was actually pushing out his own milk-white flipper, when the great truth dawned upon him that his new acquaintance sought a grip not of him but of the malacca cane. He surrendered it. The healthy barman raised it in the air.

"Well, this dings all!" he observed, in the pithy vernacular. "Do you know, sir, I had given up all hope of seeing the old gentleman's cane. So you have fallen heir to it! I congratulate you! The twenty pounds are yours!"

With that he turned towards the back of the bar, which was all glorious with bottles of cherry brandy, vodka and pansy French liqueurs. Among the bottles was a glass and in the glass an envelope, which he removed and handed to Mansie.

"Good job I'm honest," he said, "but that's my boast in this bar. Dead honest. Never gave a customer a drink I wouldn't touch myself, or a halfpenny short in the change. I've seen customers in this place, paralysed! I've see them dropping their money on the floor. I've seen them throwing it in the air like confetti. I've seen them pressing it upon me and being insulted when I wouldn't keep it. But in the morning they've all come to me and thanked me, such of them as could remember. And I ask you, why? Because I've seen them right. That's what Arthur will always do, see you right!"

"This must be Arthur," thought Mansie.

By a curious irony, one of the most advertised slogans of the insurance company was, "Jupiter Assurance will see you right!" Well, well, it was a relief to know, in this difficult world, that so many nice and influential people were prepared to see you right. But what was that about twenty pounds? Could he have heard aright? The healthy barman's conversation flowed on, as he fondled Mansie's malacca cane.

"I had a feeling the old gentleman was going to snuff it. And I make bold to guess he had the same feeling himself. He looked to me due for a thrombosis any minute. That is carrying off a good number of our customers these days. Very fashionable, of course . . . 'Arthur,' says he to me one Monday night, 'I have a feeling that the day is fast approaching when I shall have downed my last noggin. The thought causes me infinite regret, and also instils into me some envy of the ancient Vikings for the sake of their faith. What a sublime conception of paradise was that Valhalla of theirs! How easy it would be to die if one held with burning conviction that the liquor in the next world would be of even choicer quality and in unrestricted supply! Unfortunately, Arthur,' he says, heaving quite a sigh, 'I have no such delusions. I am not among those hypocrites who sigh with relief to think that all carnal appetites will be taken from them. When I go, I shall go under protest, like a man resisting arrest. And when I lie under the sod, it will be some slight relief to know that someone, somewhere, is having a damn good time.' At which I took the liberty of reminding him that he might not be capable of knowledge. 'True, Arthur,' he replied with a smile, 'you are a good Lucretian. But if we have miscalculated and by any chance I do have an inkling, it will be an enormous comfort.' So saying, he took a couple of tenners from his wallet, requested me to give him one of the management's envelopes, and having sealed them within, said, 'Arthur, when I shuffle off this mortal coil, my malacca cane will fall into other hands. Now anyone who takes a fancy to my malacca cane has a full life in store for him, and sooner or later he is bound to find his way to "The Gentleman's Lounge." You will oblige me by handing this trifling sum to whoever next enters this bar in the company of my malacca cane, with instructions to make a night of it.' Sir, here is your cane, and his envelope. What shall I pour for you?"

Mansie was just a little bombazed by this logomachy. He was staring at the envelope in stupid indecision, wondering if it could be seriously meant for him. Often the victim of practical jokes by rude fellow-clerks at the office, he naturally wondered if this could be a plant.

"Don't you believe me, sir?" said Arthur, the healthy barman. "If so, open it and see!"

Mansie tore open the flap, maintaining the malacca cane easily under one arm the while. A glorious sight, the ten-pound note of a Scottish bank, burst upon his sight like dawn in the tropics. Not for our Scottish banks the chaste and unimaginative white of the Bank of England, which is merely a superlative grade of toilet paper. No, a bold design of doubloons, crowns, coats-of-arms and scrolled legends met the eye, guaranteed by a rococo signature. From sacks of coin the sun appeared to be rising, as if suggesting that money was at the root of all pleasure and enlightenment. Mansie's first impulse was to take it home and frame it. He was recalled to his senses by the voice of the healthy barman. "There are two of them, sir."

So there were.

"What is it to be, sir?" the healthy barman continued. "May I suggest, in view of the occasion, that his own favourite tipple would not be out of place?"

Mansie did not reply for a moment. Then he merely nodded. A casual observer might have deduced that the nod denoted a dearth of original ideas. Little would he have known our Mansie! That inclination of the chin was all the outward evidence of a great decision. From now on he would drift upon the sea of life, without troubling about navigation, and allow its waves to carry him into any creeks, although not, he trusted, on to the rocks.

Arthur took several bottles from the shelf, a measure and a species of alembic. With these instruments he proceeded, not without a dazzling deftness, to conduct an experiment. While he was engaged upon it, Mansie was recalling some of the jargon of conviviality, which no one in the present age can avoid picking up from the wireless.

"Have one yourself!" he invited.

Arthur laughed gaily. "Not one of *his*, sir!" he protested. "I have my work to do. But I'll have one to celebrate your good fortune. Not one of *his*, of course! I'll rest content with a treble brandy. You quite understand, sir? I daren't take risks."

He returned to his experiment. "Good gracious me!" Mansie was thinking, in a roseate stupor. "This man talks as if treble brandies were lemonade!"

"There, sir!" said Arthur, laying a glass of yellow liquid before him. "That ought to do you good. At least it ought to do you something!"

Mansie took a sip.

"What is it?" he asked, when he recovered the power of speech. "The fission of split atoms?"

"Very good!" said Arthur, with approval. "That is the kind of compliment he might have paid me himself. It is a little receipt of my own, to which he was partial."

"What is it called?" pursued Mansie.

"I have named it the Border Widow's Lament," said Arthur.

As he toyed with the Border Widow's Lament, Mansie felt his brain to be crystal clear. He had travelled far from that woolly bewilderment in which he had frequented the Earthen Mound and drunk in the mysticism of the Children of Gabriel. Problems remained to be settled, he could not deny, but he was arranging them in an order of priority, and first on the list was undoubtedly the identity of the former owner of the malacca cane. He recalled that even in the second-hand shop the question had begun to nag him. He had put it aside as incapable of solution. Now the answer seemed within his reach.

"What was the old gentleman's name?" he asked.

Arthur looked up in surprise.

"I never knew it," he said, "but surely you must have! You being heir to the cane!"

"The cane reached me indirectly — and mysteriously," Mansie added, having had a further sip and beginning to feel that he had been granted the gift of tongues.

"This dings all!" again exclaimed Arthur. "I imagined you might be a favourite nephew. Now that I am able to size you up, I can see a strong family resemblance. To tell you the truth, I have been so much taken up with the cane that I scarcely noticed the face until this moment."

"Are you so uncivil to all your customers?"

Mansie looked round to see who had spoken and found out that it was himself. If this man in any way resembles Ned Turpin, he reflected, I am sure he will fling me out. Instead, the healthy barman was profuse and grovelling in his apologies.

"Don't misunderstand me, sir!" he besought. "I make no reflection on your face! All I meant was that catching sight so unexpected-like of such a distinguished cane —"

"Say no more!" commanded Mansie. "You merely make your offence the worse!"

Again he looked round. No one was there but himself, looking brassy. He could tell by the mirrors, from each of which he regarded himself with something very like insolence.

"Come, come, my man," he next found himself saying. "You must surely know the owner of the cane, the donor of these ten-pound notes. Come along, the change, if you please!"

Arthur paled beneath his health, and replied:

"God's honest truth, sir, I don't! Although he came in here regular, before the theatre, every Monday night."

Mansie threw back the last drops of the Border Widow's Lament, pocketed the change of one of the ten-pound notes, and with a curt nod followed the malacca cane out into the street.

Although he was unaware of it, Mansie was happiest when engaged upon a quest. He had been happy when in pursuit of the secret of the universe on the Mound on Sunday evenings. Now he had his nose on the trail again. True, this time he sought not the secret of the universe but the secret of the cane, which seemed of even greater importance. And who could have blamed him? Here was a cane, an influential cane, a formative cane, a cane both deliberative and activating. It had once acknowledged the grip of an old gentleman owing to vast expertness in matters of this life and a melancholy uncertainty, amounting to foreboding, about the next. The twinge he had felt in the second-hand shop grew more acute. A desire to track down the possessor of the malacca cane consumed him.

"But the gentleman is dead," he told himself.

"Never mind," whispered the cane. "You may still find out."

CHAPTER
SEVEN

Mansie's Revered Parent

The unknown quantity in Mansie was his father, the late Mr Magnus Thin, formerly first mate on board the mail-steamer *Fitful Head*, registered in the Port of Leith and owned by the Inchcolm and Inchmickery Steam Packet Company. Mr Thin had been drowned at sea, in catastrophic circumstances, in the very year of Mansie's birth.

We of the living sometimes treat the great army of the departed as if they were escaped convicts, and those whose taste it is to hunt them down might be likened to bloodhounds. But before the bloodhound can pursue, some personal belonging of the fugitive must be held close to its tenacious and enquiring nostrils.

The chief reason why Mansie found it so hard to envisage his deceased parent lay in the strange but undeniable fact that the flat at No. 2 Bleachfield contained no single souvenir of his existence, unless one reckoned the stout gold band that encircled the wedding finger of Mrs Thin's left hand. Of course, it was rather a long time for slippers or pipes to have lain about, but there did not even remain a sextant or a table of tides or some recognisable emblem of the late first officer's profession. Even stranger lacuna, no photographs of Mr Thin bestrewed the flat. In the houses of Mrs Thin's widowed friends the walls were almost papered with photographs of the late lamented, boyish in uniform during the first war, forbidding in the Sunday suit, uneasily gay at Oban, fatuously proud as they held high the first-born in swaddling clothes. Mansie did not conceal from himself the truth that he would have welcomed such mural decoration.

For its absence Mrs Thin offered the explanation that in her devouring grief she had been unable to tolerate the sight of any relic reminding her of the loved one. The poor cannot afford to indulge their grief so luxuriously as the rich, and in those days she was very poor. So, finding herself incapacitated for some hours by the mere sight of Mr Thin's carpet slippers, she arranged with the old clothes man to remove every garment and article of foot and head gear. Even his underwear, which might have kept her in dusters for many a day, was delivered to the ragman in exchange for a pudding bowl. Every evening, until she stuffed it in the kitchen range, she had cried her eyes out over an album which covered, in snapshots of phenomenal charm, the brief span of their lives together, from the very moment when they met at the house of a mutual friend, long since gone to his rest, until that notable day when Mr Thin was promoted first mate of the *Fitful Head*, under the command of the frequently intoxicated Captain Copinsay. From an early age Mansie was aware that, according to the unanimous testimony of the few survivors, the ongoings of Captain Copinsay had caused the disaster, and really if Mr Thin had never been promoted but had remained second mate on the *East Neuk*, it would have been one of those blessings such as Mrs Thin loved to count.

But if all the material clues had been destroyed, from the moment at which Mrs Thin observed intelligence dawning in her son, she made it her business to instil into his mind a picture of his father, of his rare and unquestioned worth, of their lambent happiness together, of the salient incidents in his promising, if abruptly terminated, career. As a child he used to sit by the fire and listen to her reminiscences. Sometimes these would concern intimate domestic matters, like what Mr Thin said to the plumber who failed in his duty, and how Mr Thin had, on his return from some second Odyssey to the Shetland Isles, praised her girdle scones. Sometimes they referred to his nautical adventures. As he grew up, she would confide in him some details of the violent and unpredictable behaviour of Captain Copinsay, of whom she would openly remark that he only kept his command by marrying the elderly sister of the managing director. Such is the value to our minds of circumstantial evidence that Mansie often found himself longing that in the general holocaust of his father's effects she had overlooked some single but significant object, such as a peaked cap with gold braid and the company's badge, by which he could have moored her accounts alongside hard reality.

Sometimes, as he sat opposite his mother at the fireside he felt as if he were listening to a fairy story, in which were recounted the exploits of that Prince Charming, his father. The years heal all wounds, and after so many years Mrs Thin could throw herself with abandon into such episodes as the wreck of the *Fitful Head* upon the Pentland Skerries. If the fairy tale could not be said to have a happy ending, at least it went out in a blaze of glory, for Mr Thin was last seen alone on the bridge, by the light of the aurora borealis, saluting as the ship plunged under. It was presumed, indeed hoped for his own sake, that Captain Copinsay had passed out.

When one came to think it over, Mrs Thin was merely the minor character who survives at the end of a classical tragedy, picking her way, alone and insignificant, through the corpses and across the smouldering embers, with every other personage knocked off. Not only were the members of her own family all dead, but the members of Mr Thin's were too. These latter could scarcely be said to have existed, for when first she knew him he was already all orphan. They had met at the house of a friend, but that friend, together with her entire family, had perished in the smallpox epidemic. Mansie believed that there did remain one or two persons upon the face of the globe who had known his father, but they were scattered abroad in such parts as New Guinea and the Aleutian Islands, and even in these days of cheap and rapid air travel never came home.

Mansie remembered asking mother, when he was still quite young, if they had always lived at No. 2 Bleachfield. She sat back, a blissful smile overspread her face and she shook her head.

"I am not saying a word against No. 2 Bleachfield," she said. "As you know, I never would. For our needs, and for our means, No. 2 Bleachfield is ideal, even if some of the neighbours are not quite — of our kind. But when your father was alive we had an even more desirable house, standing apart in its own grounds, in Murrayfield. It was situated in a very refined district, and even if the district had not been refined you would not have noticed, for a high wall enclosed the lawn, herbaceous border and rock garden. Here there was no common stair; here we enjoyed complete privacy. I can see your father now, between voyages, wearing an old Norfolk jacket and smoking a Meerschaum pipe, mowing the lawn with the razor-sharp lawn-mower which we then possessed, or kneeling beside one of the seventeen varieties of saxifrage which he had collected and which bloomed continuously throughout the summer. In those days, of course, we had dinner in the evening, and afterwards your father smoked a cigar. It was his only self-indulgence — a cigar. He was resolutely opposed to drink and gambling, and even to the incautious frittering away of money on cigarettes, but even he could not resist a cigar. But he was such a considerate man, your dear father! He knew that the smell made me a trifle faint, so he always smoked his cigar in the garden in the cool of the evening, or, if it were raining, he retired to his den. That was where he kept his charts, logs and sextants, as well as models of the ships he had sailed in, executed by old sailors inside wine bottles. The ships were in the wine bottles, you understand."

One Sunday Mansie and she chanced to be walking in Murrayfield. He recalled that this was where his parents had set up house. With lively curiosity, he asked Mrs Thin to point out to him the old homestead.

She looked uneasy for a moment.

"Did I forget to tell you?" she said at length. "The house was burned to the ground just before you were born."

What shocking news! Mansie could not have been more heavily staggered if a house had burst into flames before his eyes. Here was this charming residence, every corner of which he could visualise, with that delectable garden, swept away in another of those catastrophes which without remorse had persisted in the ruin of his luckless parents. His mother sensed his acute disappointment.

"Of course I never talk of it," she said. "It is all part of that dreadful time when in my despair I meditated upon the course of taking my life. I went out one night, feeling as if the house were a prison, and roamed the streets for many hours. Blow me if I had not left the electric iron switched on — for we possessed an infallible electric iron, although that invention was still in its infancy. When I returned, the first thing I noticed was a lurid glow in the heavens, and my ear was assailed by the fire-engine bells as the City Fire Brigade rushed all their available forces towards the conflagration. I can clearly remember being aroused from my grief, and saying to myself there must be a fire somewhere. Indeed there was! When I returned home, nothing remained of our little paradise but a heap of smoking ashes, and the seventeen varieties of saxifrage had been trampled into the mud by the boots of the firemen."

"Where was I at the time?" Mansie could not help asking, although he was surprised that his interest in the event should take such a selfish turn.

"You were not yet born," replied Mrs Thin.

"Does that mean I wasn't born till after my father was drowned?" asked Mansie. He was certain that he remembered his mother painting a tender scene in which his father had gazed down on him as he lay in the beribboned cot.

Mrs Thin was a little sharp.

"How could you have been born? I had just finished making a long cambric dress for your arrival. It was for the purpose of smoothing it that I put on the iron."

"But I thought —" began Mansie.

"If you had been born," she retorted. "You would have been in the house, and if you had been in the house, you would have come to a cruel end."

Me too, thought Mansie. The logic seemed unanswerable. So he could not visit the dear old home. Nevertheless, it would be something to visit the site and gaze upon the ruins.

"Oh," said his mother. "You can't see anything now. They carted away the stones. Our old corner is entirely occupied by new bungalows."

What diabolical frustration! Mansie became almost cross.

Still, he could console himself with the thought of the cigar. He treasured the memory because it was the solitary glimpse, as through a tiny chink in a massive wall, of father taking his pleasure. Mansie's domestic education had consisted of repeated reminders that his father always cleaned his teeth, always folded his clothes, always brushed his own shoes, never swore or lost his temper, never ran up credit, never became too intimate with neighbours but kept himself to himself, minded his own business and was of a saving disposition.

"If father was of such a saving disposition," Mansie once ventured to ask, "how does it come that we were so poor when the *Fitful Head* went down on the Pentland Skerries?"

"That is another long story," replied Mrs Thin. "You must understand that your father was a great believer in life assurance. If I go to Davy Jones' Locker, he used to say (Davy Jones' Locker being at the bottom of the sea, you understand), or if I fall a victim to any of the ills that prey upon landlubber and seaman alike, there is no comfort to the widow like a good insurance policy. In accordance with this principle, he put every penny he could save into the Rosebud Life. A very nice gentleman called once a week and took away his money, entering the total in a small black book and giving us receipts, which I preserved for years on a nail in the kitchen in case there should be any argument. But it just shows you how useless these precautions can be, for the gentleman had been putting our money into his own pocket and your father's policies were not worth the parchment they were written on."

"Scandalous!" cried Mansie. "He could never have got off with that at the Jupiter. What happened to him? Where is he now?"

"He did a long prison sentence, seven years I think, and then he sailed for America, to hide his shame in a new land. He again fell into careless ways, and the last of him was that he robbed a bank, shot the cashier, and was sent to the electric chair."

"Good gracious!" thought Mansie. "Just our family's luck! When they try to save, that's what they choose for a savings bank! It takes most of the verve out of one's good intentions. I trust the Post Office is more reliable."

Captain Copinsay, who had commanded the *Fitful Head* on that dreadful night, enjoyed a post-mortem reputation as spectacularly chequered as Mr Thin had been dependably the gentleman. Sometimes Mansie thought that his mother related the misdeeds of this navigator with a gusto unsuitable in one who had lost a beloved spouse as the direct consequence of his vagaries. Yet the sheer effrontery of Captain Copinsay was a more fruitful topic of conversation than the sober merits of his first mate. That nobody could deny. How he had obtained his master's ticket no one could understand, but there was an entertaining theory that he had bribed the examining board. He cheated the company, where possible, on stores and by taking on undeclared freight at a cheaper rate. It is a commonplace that a sailor has a wife in every port, but the Captain observed this nautical custom with his usual flamboyance by carrying on a romantic affair with the wife of the harbourmaster of Wick. After the fatal night, some support was given to the theory that the light on the Skerries did not fail by sheer accident, but that the keeper was suborned by the justly incensed harbourmaster.

The Pentland Firth is a strange and narrow sea, through which the tide swirls at twelve knots, so that many a tramp, with engines pounding, is carried in reverse. When the wind blows in one direction and the tide makes in another, the waves boil and gurgle. In the numerous tidal races, such as the Boars of Duncansby and the Wells of Swona, ships spin round and disappear, as if a plug had been pulled out at the bottom of the sea. Mermaids are often sighted, and held in conversation. Compared with these hazards, some few islands, called skerries, with rocks like the teeth of leviathans, which do not only lie in wait for ships but pursue and bite them, were of little account.

It was Captain Copinsay's favourite boast that he knew the Pentland like the back of his hand. He would sit below, a bottle of malt within his braided reach, and communicate this fact to the small gathering of hardy spirits who were keeping sea-sickness at bay. Meanwhile the faithful Thin, conning his charts and compasses, was steering the ship safe betwixt the roosts and skerries. Then came the night when there was a rude fellow in the company. Rising unsteadily to his feet, he challenged Captain Copinsay, alleging that he could not steer a toy yacht across a bathtub. At that the Captain also hoisted himself up. He mounted to the bridge and, in face of the disciplined protests of the first mate, took over the wheel. At that moment the light failed, and the skerry bit a hole in the hull of the *Fitful Head*.

The moral of this story, so far as Mansie could follow it, was that life is always fair to the vicious and foul to the virtuous, but that a certain tedious and certainly posthumous glory would accrue to those who stood firm in the path of duty. Those who fought the good fight would be rewarded with a bleak prestige and that sense of unrecognised superiority which is akin to grievance.

As he walked out from "The Gentleman's Lounge," the notes fat within his mostly scrawny wallet, Mansie's mind turned to the legend of his father. Why was he being teased with this double mystery? His life was being transformed into a quest for the identity of two men, both gone beyond recall. And even at this moment he ought to be casting a protective glance upon that silly creature who had taken her treasures of golden hair and white skin into the Osiris. The complication of life! Was there any hope of mastering it?

He had forgotten all about the cane. There it was, easy in the palm of his hand, swinging along in rhythm with his step. But suddenly it gave another of its sharpest and most peremptory tugs. He found himself leaping after it to board a tramcar. He did not even have time to read where the tram was going, but when it reached a certain point and chose one set of rails, he knew that it was bound for the ancient Port of Leith.

In a seaport any man must feel upon the veritable edge of liberation. Unlike the trim landward towns, seaports are as ill-kempt as sea-birds' nests on the cliff, mere jumping-off places. The grasp of routine and circumstance seems to slacken perceptibly as one threads one's way through narrow wynds to the harbour, guided by the salty air and the sirens of vessels which gave warning as they approach the dock gates.

All the lorries had vanished, the stevedores had gone home. Even the pigeons that have colonised the grain elevators were no longer pecking between the wagons on the rusty sidings, but had retired to roost for the night. The malacca cane led Mansie from isle to isle of lamplight and down to the quay where a notice intimated that this was the landing-stage set apart for the use of the Inchcolm and Inchmickery Steam Packet Company. One of the company's ships was tied up, without much sign of life about her except a shirt fluttering from a temporary clothesline near the fo'castle. An old man was standing on the quay, smoking his pipe. He wore the peaked cap with the company's badge, and appeared to be a caretaker.

"Fine night," said Mansie civilly.

"No that ill," replied the caretaker, not uncordially, and spat into the black and oily water.

"Were you ever a sailor?" asked Mansie.

"I have never been nothing else," the old man answered. "Man and boy I have sailed on this company's ships for sixty-three years, not a day less."

"My father!" thought Mansie. He could feel the blood racing foolishly through his head. "I am about to have news of him. Perhaps here is a survivor of the *Fitful Head*! I must be calm!"

Aloud he said, "Were you ever on the old *Fitful Head*?"

"I did fifteen years on her."

"Were you one of the survivors?"

The old sailor took his pipe from his mouth and examined Mansie with distrust.

"If you're trying to take the loan of me, you can run along," he said.

93

There is nothing offensive in suggesting that a sailor has survived a shipwreck, unless he is the captain. Mansie was bothered.

"All I mean is," he explained, "if you were fifteen years on the *Fitful Head*, you were very likely on board on that dreadful night."

"Every night I was on board the *Fitful Head* was a dreadful night."

It was Mansie's turn to look closely. Perhaps the mind was wandering.

"The night the ship foundered on the Pentland Skerries," he shouted.

"Either you're trying to be funny or you've had a dram," said the man in the peaked cap, without approval.

"Come, come," said Mansie, "don't tell me you've forgotten how the *Fitful Head* went down!"

"Very well," replied the old man, with assumed patience. "How did the *Fitful Head* go down?"

Mansie summarised the facts. The old sailor did not seem impressed.

"Let me tell you, young sir," he said with great firmness, "the *Fitful Head* never went down on the Pentland Skerries. It was purchased by the Corinth and Patmos Shipping Company and now navigates the eastern Mediterranean with consignments of Greek pilgrims. And if it's your idea of an evening's fun to come tormenting an old man with daft-like tales, I may say I think very little of it myself."

Mansie could not take it in.

"No, no," he cried. "I mean the *Fitful Head*!"

"So do I," said the sailor, and turned away.

Mansie ran after him and plucked him by the sleeve.

"The *Fitful Head* commanded by Captain Copinsay!" he added, lest by some strange coincidence there might be two ships of the same name.

"Here, you run along! I don't like you, see! There never was no Captain Copinsay in the Inchcolm and Inchmickery!"

"But you must have known Mr Magnus Thin, the first mate!"

"I never knew no Mr Magnus Thin. No, nor no Mr Magnus Thick neither! No such person never existed in no ship of this company. Buzz off!"

The cane rose dangerously in Mansie's hand, but he rode its temper out on the way back to the town. If he understood the caretaker correctly, his father had never existed.

CHAPTER
EIGHT

The Weary Pilgrimage

Mansie had need of leisure to think. Young men who want to think invariably resort to cafés, for there is nothing to be ashamed of in thinking, and if carried out publicly at corner tables it may even make one an object of interest. Besides, hunger was beginning to gnaw. Hitherto his life had been so well organised that he never felt such pangs between high tea and breakfast. When a man begins to need an extra meal, there is some reason for it. Perhaps it was the Border Widow's Lament, perhaps it was the bracing air of Leith, perhaps it was just the cane.

He sought out a restaurant on Princes Street famous for its reasonable prices and its congestion, an eating-house to which a young man might take his girl without being so beggared that she was at the mercy of his rivals for the subsequent six weeks. Mansie, although at the moment in a position to sample the best that the town could offer him, did not leave go of prudence. He entered the "Green Willow," sought a table for two, laid his coat, cap and cane across one chair, occupied the other and ordered a welsh rarebit and chips. It was the kind of place where one would have ordered chips with cherry cake. He stared at the table and concentrated upon Magnus Thin, the first mate of the *Fitful Head*. One by one the discrepancies in his mother's story began to itch like heat spots. Was he or was he not born before the death of his father? Surely one was entitled to a straightforward answer on such a point. If the house at Murrayfield had suffered such total destruction, how came it that his mother disposed of his father's wardrobe to the old clothes man? It seemed to him that his paternity was as great a take-in as the Day of Judgment, and that his own mother was no more reliable than the Children of Gabriel.

His fork was conveying the first peppery bite to his maw, when he saw a gentleman with an extraordinary quilting of clothes and an outstanding crop of hair bend over his table. Although his hair had not been clipped by the barber's shears for many a month, he was spotlessly clean. His face, unadorned except for a pair of gold pince-nez, and his long fingers, weighted by one signet ring, shone with a ghostly transparency. Mansie could see that he wore several waistcoats and a muffler as well as a heavy ulster. On his ankles were spats. Had Mansie known more of the world, he might have said "a musician."

Before he was able to think at all, the heavily clad gentleman was off like a burn in spate.

"Ah, the malacca cane, the one and only! The baton of life, I used to call it. So it is yours now! Young man, I congratulate you! A long life and a merry — that surely lies before you. Your uncle — yes, I can see you are a near relation — was a dear friend of mine. We have clashed the cymbals in our time, he and I. Alas, I am growing a little too old for it, but at least I am still capable of a convincing ping on the triangle. Many a night did I take my beat from this cane, even if I contributed some original syncopations of my own!"

He laughed delightedly at the thought. Mansie said nothing. He was baffled by this new problem, how to ask the identity of a man whom everyone assumes you must have known intimately.

The musician threw the tassel of his muffler over his shoulder and continued,

"As he left you the cane, you must be the favourite nephew, therefore I suspect you share his tastes. Well, nothing doing to-night, old man. I am on the wagon until after the recital, although when that is over — I shall probably push the boat out for a couple of days or so."

As he spoke he was fumbling in the pocket of his outermost waistcoat.

"Here is a ticket for the recital. I'm playing two of his favourite pieces —"

Mansie tried to interrupt but was waved down.

"No thank you, my dear boy, not to-night. Not on any account!"

He flexed his fingers eloquently, to the amazement of a passing waitress.

"The notes! The notes! That's what I have to keep in mind. The demi-semiquavers refuse to flow in true legato style when the giant pistons are pounding within —"

"Please, might I ask —?" began Mansie His new acquaintance clapped a hand over his mouth.

"No, no, my boy, I simply daren't listen to you. I am so weak that if you once begin your blandishments, you will prevail. So I daren't let you begin. No, no, no, I absolutely refuse to take one with you. I am off for an hour's practice. That's why I always come to this joint — it cannot be said to strive to persuade you to dally. The Mendelssohn may look easy to you. All I say is, try tackling it on top of the Bach. So, thank you very much and all that, but the answer is no, definitely no. After the recital, that will be quite a different matter. Good night!"

As he darted for the entrance, throwing a handful of small coins and his bill at the girl behind the cash desk, Mansie saw that he had dropped a piece of pasteboard on the tablecloth. He picked it up and read, "St Ninian's. Organ Recital. Algernon Plumdough, Mus.Doc., F.R.C.O.," and the date. He looked after Dr Plumdough in some dismay, but already he had vanished. The welsh rarebit had congealed. He rose, paid and again followed the malacca cane into the night.

Strolling along, Mansie reflected upon the change that was taking place in his now complicated relations with the two men whom he had never seen. As his father vanished into limbo (he would have to talk to mother about that) the old gentleman who had owned the malacca cane began dimly to materialise. He had liked the music of the organ, he had been the friend of musicians, whom he had led a merry dance. His favourite drink was to brandy as brandy is to lemon crush. He had probably succumbed to a thrombosis, which suggested an enthusiastic rather than a placid temperament. He spent his Monday nights at the theatre.

And from beyond the grave he had, by the medium of the cane, begun to assume the direction of Mansie's life.

These thoughts were taking shape in Mansie's cranium when he found himself opposite to the Mound. This being a week night, the concourse there was smaller than on the Sabbath. Nevertheless the more persistent parties and sects were out in force, each raising a minatory finger above a knot of bystanders. Another brand of hot gospellers had appropriated the stance of the Children of Gabriel. Jordan still flowed in the gutter, and the bog of sin and shame was as squelchy as ever. Looking across at them all, he suddenly found it very hard to understand what was biting them, although a month ago he had stood there yearning. When there is so much to taste and to discover here, how can they make themselves thistledown in pursuit of the hereafter. The hereafter will be upon them in its own good time, and that will be sooner than they imagine!

Good heavens, he thought, that sounds uncommonly like what my uncle might have said! And again good heavens, do I now call him my uncle? This is alarming. Yet it is true. Where is a man to begin when he cannot even solve the mystery of his own malacca cane? Certainly not at the far end of time.

He was sauntering along the pavement, on the offside so that the circles described by the malacca cane would not be broken by the figures of other peripatetic citizens. The scent of wallflowers from Princes Street Gardens, a balm of unbottleable bliss to the senses, was wafted up to him, mingled with the sulphurous reek of the steam locomotives in the Waverley Station. It was as if he trod a middle world where the perfumes of paradise combined with the fumes of the infernal regions. Suddenly a taxi drew up alongside the kerb. The door opened and from the darkness a middle-aged woman's voice addressed him in urgent tones:

"Step in! Quickly, young man! I am in a hurry and I desire to carry out business with you!"

There was a backward roll of the r's and a smooth voluptuous intonation which Mansie easily identified as French. To be asked to step into a hooded taxi-cab in the mirk of eve by a Frenchwoman — that was not the kind of invitation his mother would have advised him to accept. Even without his mother's help, he could see one or two sound reasons against it. Perhaps she kept a stiletto in her garter. On the other hand, he could not see that anyone was likely to drug him and ship him off to Buenos Ayres. To settle the matter, the malacca cane lifted perceptibly. He found himself climbing in, and drawing the door fast behind him. As the catch clicked, the taxi-driver pulled out. Inside the cab a tropical odour ruled all, and drove out the fragrant innocence of the wallflowers. Before he could properly see his companion, her voice spoke imperiously, "Let me see that cane!"

Without waiting for his permission, she seized the malacca cane. But Mansie was not to be parted from it. He hung on with all his might, and was dragged against a springy bosom as exhilarating as the turf-clad flanks of the Braids, while the lady held the knob up to such light as gleamed through the taxi window every time they passed one of the new street lamps.

101

"Yes, I thought so," she cried, somewhat relaxing her grip. "It is his cane, the malacca cane he carried everywhere! He gave me much, in the days when he loved me! But that he always refused! He would say it was not for a woman! And he has left it to you!"

She spat out these words with such ferocity that Mansie tried to lose himself in the upholstery, like some small coin. She dragged him out.

"Let me look at you, boy!" she cried. "Let me inspect you and determine what you are made of!"

She held him up to the light just as she had held the knob of the cane. He was able to study her in return. Her face was a Rubens masterpiece of rouge and powder under greying curls so neat they might have been a wig. Her greedy blue eyes glittered as bright as the pendants of brilliants that hung from her ears. She had a bosom as broad as the Paps of Fife, barely concealed by a swathe of taffeta.

"How old are you?" she snapped, throwing him down.

"Twenty-one," croaked Mansie, in strangled tones, for she had drawn his tie as tight as a hangman's noose.

"Before my time, so I suppose I ought not to object, although of course I always knew there were those others as soon as my back was turned. After all, my own fidelity was not impeccable. I am not one to overclaim. When a man goes off on a tour of the Italian Cathedrals with a bachelor friend, the woman left behind can be very lonely."

"Were you his wife?" asked Mansie, still dizzy from his strangling and the mental agility required by her statements. The lady laughed so that all her flesh heaved and the springs of the taxi squeaked under her.

"Ah, you are so sweet, so young!" she exclaimed. "You are like a little souvenir of my past. I will keep you. You will stand upon the mantelpiece, between a shepherdess and a Chinese mandarin, and every time I look at you you will, despite your innocence, remind me of him. You are absurd! I love you!"

She hugged Mansie to her bosom and smothered him in kisses. Yes, smothered is the word, smoored, almost overlaid, as if he had been a helpless infant. He was too desperately engaged in fighting for his life to feel embarrassed. The drowning man is not especially worried because he feels his bathing trunks slip off.

"Oh, I plan a big, big treat for you," she sighed, sinking back into a corner so that the cab canted over as if a spring had broken. "You come with me to the Osiris. You have tasted the champagne, eh?"

"No," cried Mansie. He meant that he would not darken the doors of the Osiris, but she took him up on the champagne.

"What? Never? Ah, there is nothing that so appeals to an ageing woman as to give a young man his first sip of champagne! What pleasure this affords!"

Again Mansie strove to make his protest. Again she missed the point.

"You say I am not ageing? Oh, you are a flatterer, just as he was! But I am ageing. You see, I can face the truth. Some fools will tell you that we all age from the cradle on. My dear, it is not so. That is a miserable attempt to console oneself against the true approach of age. No, no, we grow, we mature and then we age, and when we age, not all the stoics can make it good. It is not even consolation if we can say upon oath that we have done as we pleased, for we shall never do it again, and how bitter is that reminder. Yet some vicarious joys persist. To pour your first champagne, to watch the bubbles break against those lips that have never been caressed by wine, but have only suffered the harsh and tannic assault of over-brewed Indian tea — ah yes, something truly persists. You will be my rose in December!"

"No, no," began Mansie, for the last time. She enveloped him in a vast maternal kiss, without passion but full of an inexplicable fondness. That kiss really did it. If every time he attempted a protest he was to be hugged, stifled and asphyxiated, then it was wiser to abandon the struggle. As soon as he ceased to fight, the sense of panic began to leave him. There was the malacca cane between his fingers, smooth and reassuring. The thought of the Osiris might terrify him out of his wits, but the cane was in no degree unnerved. This is very foolish of me, thought Mansie. I may have to forget father for the time being. In fact I am rather relieved to, for I do not look forward to the scene with mother. But at least I can push on with the enquiry about uncle. I wish I could find someone to believe I don't even know his name. That was when it occurred to him that, as so often in life, the indirect approach was to be preferred.

"Madam," he said with the utmost courtesy, "would you consider it impertinent of me to enquire your name?"

"Why, of course not, Mr Kincaid," she graciously replied.

Once again Mansie felt as if he had lost contact with the earth. Kincaid? That was not his name. Yet she uttered it as if it were on his birth certificate.

"Kincaid?" he said. "That is not my name, madam!"

"So?" she ejaculated, then patted his hand in a motherly way. "Of course. I should have known. Well, I am the last person in the world who says a thing like that with the intention to offend. If by chance you are offended, I immediately ask your pardon. But you will tell me, my little one, by what name you call yourself."

"Thin," said Mansie, trying to give the name a dignity it did not possess, "Magnus Thin."

She considered for a moment.

"I am glad of the Magnus," she said. "I am glad he gave you that. I shall call you that. But the Thin — no, he never mentioned her. Of course, before my time, and when one is on with the new love, why should anyone waste time talking of the old."

Perhaps this woman is a lunatic, thought Mansie. Although the cane stood firm, he glanced with some apprehension from the window. They were by now beyond the West End, and jolting over the setts in the direction of Murrayfield.

"Do you not wish to know *my* name?" she suddenly asked, with such an expression of outraged dignity that he quickly told her he did.

"My true name — no man knows it. But like the rest, you will call me Madame Désirée!"

Was there to be no end to these staggering blows? So this was the customer who thought Myrtle a nice girl and threw her into the arms of American sailors! The taxi slowed down and turned sharply in at the gate of a large stone villa with rhododendrons growing beside the drive. The portico of the house was flooded with light. Inside the door Mansie caught a glimpse of potted palms and garish scarlet flowers. A footman in chocolate livery, chocolate top-hat and white gloves advanced. Mansie sat tight, waiting for Madame Désirée to dismount.

"You get out!" she ordered. "The gentleman always dismounts first from a carriage, then offers his hand to the lady. You are very green. I shall have to lend you Lady Troubridge's 'Book of Etiquette.' In some respects it is out of date, as when it forbids unmarried women to travel in lifts with strange men. Your arm, if you please."

On the gravel, as the chocolate footman moved ceremoniously ahead, Madame Désirée paused and looked up at the front of the villa, so boot-faced and shuttered by comparison with the gaping invitation of the portico.

"You recognise it, yes?" she enquired.

Mansie quickly scanned the well-dressed stone, but could see nothing to recognise. He shook his head.

"He left it to me in his will. Little enough! But who looks a gift horse in the mouth for long? I had an idea. I had scraped a little together over the years. Gentlemen had given me presents, you know. I always had them valued at the time, but since those days their value has trebled. Ah well, they are now in America, I suppose. At least I have been able to start my little dance club. I am doing well. The place is gay. And he would have been amused — oh, more than amused, my little friend, he would have tumbled down with laughing!"

"But who was 'he'?" asked Mansie, in utter bewilderment.

For a second Madame Désirée lost her benignity. She stamped her foot.

"You really are a stupid boy!" she cried. "I am talking of your father!"

The storm was over as quickly as it had blown up. She gripped him by the arm, stared at his face and made the noise of a thousand doves cooing together deep down in her throat.

"You really are a stupid boy," she crooned, "but you are irresistible! You are so young, so innocent, your eyes are so big, like saucers, and your face wears an expression of almost perpetual astonishment. As you are now, so must he have been at the age of twenty-one! Come with me!"

She led him into the carnival of flowers.

CHAPTER
NINE

Pleasure Dome

Madame sailed under bellying canvas into the entrance
hall, sweeping on Mansie in her progress, as if he were
a dinghy tied to her counter. Beneath the glittering
chandelier she cast him off. A broad stairway led
forward and upward, and the clans were gathering, for
men and women passed up it in a steady stream. Outside
the ladies' cloakroom, squires champed impatiently until
their ladies appeared. As he stood gripping his cane like
a sheet anchor, Madame Désirée said:

"Put your things in the cloakroom! Then come straight
to the office!"

She went straight to a door marked "Private," opened
the door with a latch-key from her handbag, and
disappeared within.

Now is my chance, thought Mansie. I shall flee. I shall
dart suddenly, with the acceleration of a greyhound. I
shall pass the chocolate uniform with all the relentless
force of the one o'clock train passing Linlithgow. I shall
jink him in the rhododendrons if need be. Then I shall be
out in the free air of Murrayfield, and once again under
the comforting supervision of the Edinburgh police. He
turned, saw that the door was clear, gathered his sinews

for the great effort and sprang. But he had reckoned without the malacca cane. It remained staunch, so that it seemed to be buried ten feet deep in concrete. The severe jar made his very skeleton rattle. He sighed but did not question the cane. It inclined a little towards the door marked "Cloaks — Gentlemen." He went obediently towards it, and found it opened upon a stair leading to the basement, in the ambages of which Madame Désirée had situated the offices necessary for the entertainment of large numbers of guests.

During the descent to these lower regions, Mansie strove hard to adjust his mind to his new situation. Despite all the evidence to the contrary, he was unable to rid himself of the belief, implanted into him by his mother from his earliest years, that his father was a good and true man named Magnus Thin. Yet there now appeared to be a substantial mound of evidence that his father was in unsober fact a Bohemian gentleman known as Magnus Kincaid to a disreputable old Frenchwoman. There could be little doubt that he had inherited the cane from Mr Kincaid, in however roundabout a fashion, and equally that the cane had become a tutor charged with his further education. As for Mr Kincaid himself, Mansie's mind quailed before the flame-shot splendours and enigmas of his character.

Mansie passed swiftly by the entrance to a porcelain lavatory where several sailors of the matriarchal transatlantic states were imbibing from hip-flasks sufficient courage to brace them for a large scale revenge upon strange women. Already they were beginning to talk in a boastful yet self-pitying way. One of them caught sight of Mansie, threw an empty bottle at him with all his force, laughed genially, then fell in a heap on the tiles. The cane drew Mansie to one side just in time and the bottle splintered on the wall behind his ear. A walk-on from *Aïda* appeared with a brush and shovel to remove the traces. Mansie hurried on towards the counter marked "Cloaks."

His attention was still drawn to the rear, for it is always well to be on the look-out for flying bottles. He slipped off his overcoat and laid it beside his cap and muffler on the counter. An elderly woman in a white overall was enclosed in this cave of hat-pegs to receive the clothes and to hand out tickets. As she stretched out her hand, her attitude stiffened and she let out a tiny cry. Mansie, who could not spare attention for her till then, now looked hard at her. He almost dropped. It was his mother, Mrs Thin.

What a torrent of blame and admonition would now rush over him! Mansie dreaded scenes, more he dreaded scenes in front of strangers, most of all he dreaded scenes with his mother. If only the earth would open and swallow him up. He clung to the valiant cane for dear life.

To his amazement Mrs Thin averted her eyes, in an uncontrollable admission of guilt, which caused him to stare at her as if she had grown an extra nose.

"Here is your ticket, sir," she said in a quavery voice, and instantly retired to the most distant point of her lair. Mansie had not yet parted with the malacca cane. It now occurred to him that it would be a little unusual not to give it up. He held it out, in a hesitant way. Mrs Thin caught the gesture from the corner of her eye. Her expression of guilt changed to one of hatred and she returned eagerly towards him.

"I will take your cane, sir," she croaked.

Mansie withdrew it as he understood the gleam in her eye, but she had hold of the end of it. For a moment they hauled savagely in a tug-of-war across the counter, then the cane slithered in her fingers and with a wrench Mansie was able to drag it free.

"I think I shall keep my cane after all!" he remarked as if nothing had happened.

Her "Just as you please, sir," was as rigidly controlled, but no effort could screen the mortified frustration in her eyes.

Mansie retreated rapidly towards the stairs. The sailors were reviving their comrade with pellets which were issued to them for their shore leave and did all but bring the dead to life. But in face of the greater peril Mansie would have cared nothing for the whole American fleet with its guns blazing.

That single expression in Mrs Thin's eye had admitted everything. The great imposture was now plain. There had never been a hero of the name of Magnus Thin, there had never been the perfect husband, the considerate man about the house, the copy-book father, worthy of being imitated in every particular of conduct by the true son. He was a figment, a fantasy without flesh and blood. And yet Mansie could see him clearly, on the bridge of the *Fitful Head*, with head erect and hand at the salute, at that moment of time before the wounded ship was dragged beneath the surging Pentland waters. There was only one minor difference. The countenance of the noble first mate wore an air of resignation even more profound than a martyr's, for he knew that his sacrifice was of no avail.

Was Mrs Thin his mother after all? Had she merely abstracted him from a perambulator in a fit of maternal kleptomania? If she were his mother, what was the secret of his birth about which she had practised such systematic deception? All his affection for her rose suddenly into the air like a sea mist and permitted him a brief vision of her without the filial haze. She seemed to be a remarkable old hypocrite. How she would have loved to make away with the malacca cane, to chop it in a thousand pieces and incinerate it! If that vagrant, free-thinking cane had fallen into her hands, it would have lived to strut no more.

He now stood before the door of the room marked "Private." The cane rapped sharply thrice, at which a voice full of suspicion enquired who was there. The question placed Mansie in an awkward situation. He had disproved his own identity so convincingly that he was far from certain. This was one of the important split seconds in his life, because instead of weeping he smiled. Oh, the divine moment when a man who might well pity himself is moved instead to laughter!

"I don't quite know!" he called out gaily.

The door opened and Madame Désirée beamed out without a hint of the suspicion that had tinged her question with hostility.

"I always ask before I open," she said, "in case it should be the police. Come in, my little friend! Ah, the likeness, in the stronger light! See what I have found for you!"

Mansie saw a black evening suit folded over the back of a chair, a stiff shirt with a starched front like a beautiful sea-shell, patent leather shoes and shiny black silk socks.

"These belong to Peter," said Madame Désirée, "but as he will not be out of Saughton for another year, I should consider them yours for the time being. Besides he has cheated me out of twice their value. He is precisely your build and height."

"You don't mean me to put these on?" asked Mansie. He leaned heavily upon the cane, and required all the support it could give.

Madame Désirée shrugged and exposed the palms of her chubby hands as if he were a child who refused to be convinced of the obvious.

"My dear boy, you are dressed as if this were an insurance office. It is not. You will change."

"Very well," he replied, wisely understanding that he was being given no option. "But where?"

"Here!" said Madame Désirée, sweeping her arm round the room as if it were the Usher Hall.

Mansie felt the cold and prickly hand of fright on the nape of his neck. He glanced round the room. It was a mixture of place of business and boudoir, with a divan, that aroused his basest suspicions, in one corner. The air was laden with perfume and the aroma of Egyptian cigarettes. He could feel it coming. Yet he clung to a straw of hope.

"I don't like to ask you to leave —" he ventured.

Madame Désirée beamed.

"You do not have to, my child, because I am going to stay. Do not be scared. I will not devour you. I might take you on my knee and stroke your hair, but I would not devour you."

Mansie was not reassured. Like most human beings, he was more devoted to his clothes, particularly the outward and visible layer, than a hermit crab to its shell. He had nothing to be ashamed of in the condition of his underwear. Mrs Thin kept them spotlessly clean, on the assumption that anyone at any time may be run over by a bus and exposed to stripping by complete strangers. His feet and knees, also, could have borne immediate inspection.

Madame Désirée pointed to an elegant French screen, which he had not observed because it was pushed behind a filing cabinet.

"I do not understand you," she said. "When I was your age, I loved to undress. But there is a screen, if it will spare your blushes."

Mansie drew out the screen from behind the cabinet and extended its three sections to make a little bathing hut for himself. It was a genuine French screen, for it revealed too much, having been designed for use in French bedroom farces so that the shoulders of the leading lady might be admired as she changed her dress. Mansie felt in a horribly vulnerable position as he unbuttoned his braces, but his fears left him as Madame Désirée showed no disposition to take advantage of it. She sat at her bureau and prattled, as with half her attention and a gold fountain pen she signed a pile of cheques.

"Of course you do not dance. You glide about in a dream. You are a noctambulist, my young friend. You bump and are bumped. Sometimes you wake from your trance. Then you are terrified because what was present is absent, and all around is strange and different. Yet it is only a different part of the same forest, as they say in plays, and you are still a lost baby. A rumba band is an expensive luxury."

Her last observation was prompted by the cheque then under her hand. Mansie at that juncture resembled a snake that has just sloughed its skin. He was thankful when she continued:

"You do not dance. But all men and women must learn to dance. Otherwise they bruise and are bruised. Who can tell why all this dancing must go on? The stars dance all night to their own music in a stupid and distant way, like German margraves with their margravines. I am sure they do not know why they do it, but at least they avoid collisions. Nor do I know why men and women have to dance. I have observed that they must. That is all. I do not believe in drinking gin, but I am obliged to keep it for the sake of the barbarians."

As she rambled on, dividing her mind between metaphysics and finance, Mansie was donning his new clothes. The socks, shoes and trousers gave no trouble, being very much the same old one-and-sixpence as before. By intellectual foresight rather than trial and error he struck the great truth that it is best to insert the links before donning the shirt. But when he reached the white bow-tie his inexperience caught up with him.

"Let me!" said Madame Désirée, as, leaning against the screen, she knotted the bow with a few twirls of her fingers, drew it tight and straightened the ends. What a truly accomplished woman, thought Mansie. He was just putting on the tail-coat, which sat nicely over his shoulders and rump, when she startled him again.

"For the dancing," she said, "I think I shall turn you over to Julie. Julie would meet your case, I think."

To Mary, to Jessie, that would have been sufficiently alarming, but to Julie — no young man at the threshold of his career could regard the thought of being turned over to Julie with anything but the fear that he might not be able to weather it. Yet, when Madame Désirée was decided upon anything, protests were reduced to an undignified waste of time. So he clutched the cane, which seemed quite unperturbed, and waited.

Madame Désirée pressed a key on her desk telephone and commanded to the empty air:

"Send down Julie and a bottle of champagne!"

Then turning to Mansie, she added with a smile, "We could have had a magnum, but it is a mistake to overdo anything the first time. It will be my own champagne too, not what they serve at the tables. I don't suppose you could tell the difference, but as one grows older, *mon dieu*, how one can tell the difference! My boy, as the years knit up, life may become simpler but it also becomes more expensive. The world seems so much fuller of the inferior article than when one was young.

Besides, it is important for me to set you a high standard, on grounds of abstract principle."

Mansie was little interested in grounds of abstract principle.

"Who is Julie, perhaps I really mean what is Julie?" he said.

"Julie is a professional dancer. One of my best girls. She could infuse a sense of rhythm into a Writer to the Signet. Boy, what is your profession or trade?"

Mansie told her that he was a clerk in an insurance office.

"We must cure you of that," was her only comment.

The door opened and Julie stood framed there a heartbeat or two before entering. She was a beautiful girl, not too tall, and when she moved it was with the slow sinuosity of a priestess of some Eleusinian cult. There was in her too a passivity and repose which gave her an air of rapt distance, for in his individual, protestant and self-determining city Mansie had never encountered the servant of a mystery. Behind Julie walked a eunuch carrying a bottle of iced champagne within a silver pail.

"Julie, this is Mr Magnus Kincaid. My child, this is Mademoiselle Julie."

He was about to stretch out his hand for a firm handclasp *à l'écossaise*, when she inclined her head. It was her acknowledgment of him, yet he wondered if she were not also trying to conceal an expression both servile and amused.

"Draw the cork!" Madame instructed the waiter. "We shall take a glass. Then, Julie, you will teach Magnus to dance. How can they call a baby Magnus! They should call him first Parvus, then one day he would blossom into Magnus. *Votre santé!* We shall see you a true Magnus before we have done with you!

Mansie was by no means a connoisseur of fine wines. At the New Year his mother was wont to lay in the traditional bottle of Empire Port. On the whole, he preferred it to the bottle of beer which Mr Clague had once pressed upon him at the same promiscuous season, offering, by way of encouragement, to knock him into the middle of next week if he did not drink it. He had also suffered whisky in therapeutic doses. He could not have said that he was enthusiastic about any of them. He had always thought, however, that perhaps it might be different with champagne.

It is impossible to be quite sure of what Mansie expected to taste in his first sip of champagne. Mortals may only venture rough guesses at the flavour of the food of the gods. For instance, many maintain that ambrosia must have resembled the delicious sweetmeat "halva" which one may eat in Greek restaurants, a probable theory at least, since the gods were, after all, Greek themselves. But these matters are subjective. Grown men have confessed that their idea of nectar was raspberry vinegar as it tasted in their childhood but had never tasted since. A child's delight on an adult palate — perhaps.

This much is certain. Nectar and champagne were thoroughly confused in Mansie's mind, and when he had drunk a single mouthful he felt mildly disappointed. He had not expected it to possess the rich and vulgar fruitiness of the Empire Port, but yet he felt entitled to expect some other quality infinitely more delightful but as easily grasped. It was light, dry, brisk but not, in his opinion, something to make all that fuss about. Perhaps it was just another of those symbols which were created out of nothing by convention, like the emperor's new clothes. At least I can drink plenty of this innocuous liquor, he told himself with relief. For example, I could drink that whole bottle. I expect it is like cider and does not count as a drink. It slips down easily, that I should be the last to deny.

"You like it, eh?" asked Madame.

"It is an agreeable wine," said Mansie, full of the confidence which his sense of capacity gave him. He had never felt like this about Empire Port.

"Another glass?"

"If you please, Madame Désirée."

"Perhaps I ought to have called for the magnum after all. Julie, pour a glass for him!"

With old-fashioned courtesy Mansie was about to save her the bother, but Madame Désirée bade him desist.

"No, no, a gentleman should never have to help himself. He should always be helped. Right up, Julie!"

This is the life, thought Mansie. Events were again given a fresh turn by the decisive Madame Désirée. She sat down abruptly at her bureau and said to Julie: "Now I have a letter to write. Pay no attention to me. He is all yours."

She snapped down a key on her desk telephone and instantly from the loud-speaker of the instrument came the music of the band in the ballroom above. They were playing a tango. The slow throb filled the little private office. Mansie looked at Julie and in less than a minute he was under.

Julie was, among other things, an expert hypnotist. The gift came to her from nature and made her quite supreme as a teacher of dancing. Madame had watched the tautness of Mansie's body relax under the influence of the good wine, and with unerring skill passed him on to her assistant. Mansie was only conscious of two deep eyes glowing at him from behind a glass of champagne. With her hand she made some few magic passes in front of his eyes, stepped close to him, and pressed his right hand round her waist. She continued to peer into his eyes. They began to sway.

How elementary, by comparison with Julie's art, are the cantrips of those mesmerists who render their subjects ridiculous by the suggestion that they are riding on horseback or fly-fishing! She was able, by the mere communication of eye and limb and pressing hand, to control his gangling movements and to guide them to the rhythm of the tango. At first she was content to let him sway. It was as if a plaster cast in an art gallery were gradually coming to life. All the time the tango throbbed like the pulse of some larger being. Back and fore, back and fore, with more and more willowy bendings, yet the feet were still anchored to the plinth. Then the heels were away and only the toes left tugging in a quagmire of immobility. At last they too were loose. Mansie was dancing!

Up and down they moved before the desk of Madame Désirée, who never looked up from her letter. Gradually steps were succeeded by glides, glides by rhythmic stampings and these by double stampings, and the double stampings by beats cunningly missed so that the boy could bend low against the girl. Mansie was dancing!

At last Julie spoke, close in his ear. She had a voice like wood smoke against a tree-clad hillside on a summer evening, with trout jumping in the loch and the Atlantic far away.

"You can dance," she said. "You can always dance! What I have given you, none can take away from you. You will never hear music now but your feet and body will desire to move in unison with it. Whatever the beat, follow it! Whatever the mood, surrender to it!"

She made a few more magic passes, and Mansie began to return to his senses as if from the embrace of some delightful new anaesthetic. His sensations were of one who has not only lost all clumsiness but who has at the same time been freed of the restrictions of the law of gravity. They danced for some moments together, then the tango came to an end. Madame Désirée snapped off the loud-speaker.

"You show promise," she remarked.

"Can I go back now, Madame?" asked Julie. "I am heavily booked."

"All right. You're a good girl. Have some champagne. And take Mr Kincaid up with you."

Mansie had laid down the malacca cane while practising the tango, but he now picked it up.

"You cannot take a malacca cane into a ballroom," cried Madame. "I will take care of it for you."

"I bet you would, if I gave you half a chance," retorted Mansie, to his own amazement, "but I am afraid I do not trust you that far, Madame Désirée. My malacca cane and I do not part company so easily!"

Madame Désirée burst into tears of rage.

"Ingrate! Codfish! Heartless wretch!" she cried, tearing bundles of cheques in her excitement and sending them flying round the room. "You take all and give nothing! You grind a poor old woman into the asphalt! Did I wonder if you were a man or a baby? You are a man, full-grown and complete, because you are brutal, selfish, intractable, cunning, self-centred, merciless. But I adore you! Would that I were young again, that I might become your victim!"

Julie had finished her glass of champagne. She was unmoved by this exhibition of feminine temperament.

"Will I take him up now?" she asked.

"Drown him if you wish!"

"You had better come with me," said Julie.

As Mansie followed her from the room, patting the cane affectionately, Madame Désirée called after them.

"Remember, Julie, he is to pay for nothing! Tell Alois it will be all right. And come back to see me, my child. I beg you, for your vile father's sake, come back to see me!"

CHAPTER
TEN

One Foot of Cold Steel

Julie and Mansie mounted the staircase with a current of cold air behind them. The brass instruments of the band were playing softly and languorously with mutes, so that the shuffle of the dancers' feet across the floor of the ballroom sounded like part of the orchestration. Julie, with sure instinct, paused in the doorway of the ballroom to allow her companion to receive and to absorb the shock of this new spectacle.

Mansie saw a chamber of amazing and unsuspected size to be contained in a private villa. In fact, several partitions had been knocked down, leaving the ceiling to be supported by four slender pillars now encrusted with gilt foliage and adorned with winged Cupids. At one end the small but ample band was raised aloft on a species of altar. Through the gloom of the dimmed lights Mansie noted the figure of Dr Algernon Plumdough bent over the keys of the piano. He was not really surprised; indeed he had reached that stage of wonder when surprise becomes an undesirable and even vulgar reaction, betraying a man unversed in the world and its manifold marvels. Whenever he accomplished a solo break, Dr Plumdough beat the piano with frenzy. He did not coax it, but dug in the spurs and rode it hell for leather.

At the other end of the room, part of the wall was occupied by a bar of extreme luxuriance on which the coloured bottles of undrinkable liqueurs and *apéritifs* stood rank upon rank like hothouse flowers. There were silver cocktail shakers and crystal and silver bowls of ice. Everything was done up regardless, but when he looked at the face of the barman, Mansie winced. It was none other than Ned Turpin. Ned seemed to feel eyes upon him, for at that instant he looked up from his shaker, caught sight of Mansie, and ground his teeth. Mansie turned away.

A master of ceremonies was bearing down upon him. Julie advanced and whispered in his ear. This was Alois. At first he seemed disposed to be argumentative, but before long he switched a subservient smile across the darkness of his countenance.

"Mr Kincaid, I am happy to welcome you," he said, "but you will not take me amiss, I trust, when I say that a malacca cane is a little out of place in a crowded ballroom. I shall be happy to take it from you."

"How do you know I have not an artificial limb?" asked Mansie.

"Sir, I apologise," said Alois with a bow. "Forgive me — but they do these things so well nowadays one can scarcely tell the true from the false. I can foresee the day when we shall have artificial hearts, lungs and stomachs as well as teeth and limbs. Shall we then remain human? It is, sir, a question I often ask myself. You are the guest of Madame Désirée. Have what you will, a bottle of wine, any delicacy you care to choose from the cold buffet. The caviare is recommended, also the fat pandores, which we illicitly dredge from the Forth. The partners are also at your service should you wish to dance, but I shall esteem it a favour if you will not permit the cane to become entangled in the limbs of the other dancers."

With a bow, Alois departed. Julie had been claimed by her American, who kept winking to his friends as he trotted round.

Mansie was still gazing in wonder at the scene from the doorway when whom should he detect among the dancers but Mr Woodburn, his boss at the Jupiter Assurance. He was clinging to a plump little redhead in bottle-green taffeta and nuzzling in her prickly hair. Mr Woodburn was a tall man in the office, but to get down to the redhead he had to bunch himself almost double. He was a strange sight. Not till he passed quite close was Mansie able to identify him beyond possibility of error, by means of a mole on his left ear. So may one recognise corpses horribly mutilated and decayed.

This indeed shows me a new aspect of the general manager, thought Mansie. It was my general impression that he considered life must not only be insured by the Jupiter but dedicated to it. The Jupiter I imagined to be his Moloch or Dagon, but here he is at a different shrine. I trust he does not see me. It will do my career no good.

Just at that moment Mr Woodburn and the redhead came round again. He must have been guiding her largely by instinct, for he was burrowing in the girl's thick curls like a dog that has lost a bone. As they slid

125

past Mansie a second time, he raised his eyes and spotted Clerk Thin. The recognition was instantaneous, but for a space of seconds the improbability delayed Mr Woodburn in awarding it the sanction of his intellect. Then he went a bright scarlet and began to whisper excitedly in the redhead's ear. She turned and studied Mansie not without interest, then with her partner broke loose from the dance. She went and sat by herself in the corner, while Mr Woodburn straightened up and strolled in Mansie's direction.

"Fancy seeing you, Thin, old fellow!" he said, with a good appearance of unconcern. "Delightful place this! Quite a change from the office. I don't often come here of course. Have a drink with me, old chap!"

"Won't your friend feel lonely?" asked Mansie.

"Oh, her?" said Mr Woodburn. "I want you to know that isn't a friend. She's a niece, from Tillicoultry, who insists upon a little gaiety when she comes to town."

Just then an American sailor passed behind Mansie, remarking "Sez you!" as part of quite another conversation. Mr Woodburn, whose eyes had been lingering on the redhead, turned sharply, as if stabbed.

"You're right, Thin!" he said quite humbly. "You're dead right. It won't wash. Come to the bar and I'll tell you quickly. Yes, yes, my dear fellow! What is it to be? Champagne? Very well, barman, two glasses of champagne."

Ned Turpin growled as he served the order, but Mansie kept to leeward of Mr Woodburn and listened with courtesy to his outpourings.

126

"I know what you think," he began, "for I know what I should have thought when I was your age had I seen a man in his late fifties make a fool of himself over a piece like that. In ten years she will be as ugly as a toad, she is even now as mercenary as an automatic till, and she is incapable of ignoring even one of the higher apes if he glanced in her direction. Yet I adore her. I am crazy about her. She is giving me something so like my youth all over again that I can forgive everything. Ah, my young friend, I have spent a lifetime in the assurance business, but at the end of a long career I recognise that you cannot insure against death. You may take yourself a ticket in the great tontine, but it is your widow who has a beanfeast on the proceeds. I am nearing the allotted span for high executives, which according to our statistics is somewhat briefer than the term biblically specified. Women — from them at first we take our fire, they cool it when it burns intolerably, and in the end of the day they are the wind that blows upon the embers as they fall apart and conceal the absence of fresh fuel. Pity yet envy an old man's love. It is shameless and shameful, clear-sighted yet delirious, it has all youth's ardour without youth's self-delusion. You don't know what I'm talking about, do you? May you never! May a tree of the forest blow over and squash you ere you come to my pass. For I love you, young boy. And I'm not drunk, if that's what you're thinking. If only I can last out two more years at the Jupiter! You will keep quiet about this, won't you? I'll see you don't suffer for discretion. Oh my God!"

He gave a little hurt squeal as he glanced for the seventieth time in the direction of the redhead.

"Look at her!" he cried. "She has hooked an American sailor. In less time than it has taken me to put you in the picture. Why did I come here? It will take me the whole night to buy back my little toffee!"

He rushed away. At that moment the dancing stopped, for an American sailor had suddenly stood up in the middle of the floor. He was taking handfuls of dollar bills from his pockets and scattering them about, while he kept shouting, "It's mine! It's mine! If it isn't mine already, I'm buying it now, see?"

I suppose the Russians are really much worse, sighed Mansie to himself. The band had stopped playing, and were crawling about on the floor, led by Dr Algernon Plumdough, in search of dollars. Other natives, who had been dancing, joined in the scramble so that soon there was not a note to be seen. Women seemed a little fuller bosomed and several men had bulging pockets. That was all the difference. The sailor was now sitting on the floor crying.

"I'm really a helluva nice guy," he wailed. "Wouldn't kill a cockroach. Yet anybody would think I stank."

"You've said it, Teddy!" several of his compatriots agreed, and began to carry him out. The Rumba Band, swarthy and cynical, now took the place of the Plumdough ensemble, who were crowding round the bar.

"Good evening, Doctor," said Mansie, observing the Mus.Doc. at his elbow. "You didn't tell me that you were going to beat it out four in the bar."

Dr Plumdough clapped his hand over Mansie's mouth.

"Hush," he said, "they think here that my name is Al Sauerpuss, that my father was born in Chicago, of German parents, and had a liaison with a negress from New Orleans, of which I am the outcome. You see, in this part of my existence I profess both the Chicago and the New Orleans styles, so I thought it best to arrange residential qualifications when I was about it. You cannot understand what my life here means to me. I was a child prodigy. At eleven I knew the entire works of Bach and could improvise fugues like nobody's business. Ah, how I used to envy those who did not find their accomplishments easy to gain. But that is by the way. My real grievance went deeper. You see, my dear boy, I have always believed that music was frenetic in purpose. That is why, unlike many of my fellow musicians, I have always regarded the Highland bagpipe as the finest instrument on God's earth. Men will advance into a hail of bullets and never feel the lead when they hear the scale of A minor played upon it."

"Scotsmen will," Mansie felt obliged to correct.

"Yes, and apparently Gurkhas, not to mention the warlike Moslems of Pakistan. But I mentioned the bagpipes purely by way of illustration. Dance music is also frenetic. My dear chap, you cannot possibly understand how frightfully boring it is to be a classical executant, particularly upon the church organ, even the remarkably fine four-manual example over which I — or should I say that fellow Plumdough — presides at St Ninian's. The critics come and sit at my recitals with their heads on their bosoms like sleeping pelicans. The next day I read that they liked my registration in the Reger, or that the second subject of the Bach would have sounded better on the trumpet stop. That sort of thing leaves one profoundly discontented. But here I rouse them, I stir the depths of their being. My piano will make love for them like the castanets of a Spanish dancer chattering together. They cannot tell if I am playing in the key of C or G. Indeed they might be vastly astonished to learn I was playing in any key at all. But their silly little hearts beat to my tempi. I can make them melancholy, erotic or even, dare I say it, happy."

He turned to Ned Turpin and shouted in a crude middle Western voice, "Say, son, set up a couple rye high-balls and make it snappy!"

He turned to Mansie and whispered, "I have to do this. They would never believe I could play if I didn't."

Mansie had lost some of his original interest in the musical dilemmas of Dr Plumdough because his anxiety on one point was mounting to the proportions of a fever. Where was Myrtle? When he had seen her at the outset of his experiences, she had been on her way to the Osiris, by the special invitation of Madame Désirée. At first he had supposed her to be lost in the crush, one of the crowd of dancers which circled and ever circled. But as his eye became accustomed to the twilight and more carefully screened the revolving couples, he became convinced that she was not in the ballroom. The Mus.Doc. was in the midst of a lengthy meditation on the age-old connection between music and the dance, and primitive religion and fertility cults, when Mansie interrupted him.

"Anywhere else? Anywhere else in these exclusive premises? Well, my dear fellow, she might be dining in one of the private rooms. They're very snug in there, I do assure you!"

A week or two before that date, had he heard that Myrtle was dining in private with an American sailor, he would have turned up his nose and said "Very likely!" Now began a great suffering, which made him think kindly of Mr Woodburn. A jealous possessiveness lodged in his bosom like a red-hot stone. Why have I been so blind, he demanded of himself. There she has been all these years, on the same stair, and I had only begun to notice her, although she is probably the greatest beauty in the world to-day. Nor had I noticed till now her exceptionally beautiful, simple and trusting nature, which is an unfortunate nature for any girl to possess in these times except where men like me are in question. She may not know it, she may not want it, but she needs protection. He grasped the cane firmly, resolved to inspect the private rooms and take charge of Myrtle, if it were not too late.

That was when Myrtle emerged from a door quite close to him, fleeing like a Bacchante with her hair tousled and a slight tear in the shoulder strap of her dress. She was being pursued by a juvenile gorilla who was crying in a vexed voice, "I paid for your supper, didn't I?"

At that point Myrtle caught sight of Mansie.

"Oh, Mansie, save me! I thought he wanted to talk about home!" she cried and hid behind him.

"Out of my way, louse!" said the sailor.

Mansie raised the stick to prod him away. The sailor snatched at the stick and gave it a twist, to wrench it from Mansie's hand. But instead of disarming Mansie, as it is to be feared he had the strength to do, he armed him more dangerously. For there was a click and the entire cane slipped away, leaving Mansie presenting a foot of cold steel. For this excellent malacca cane was, if not a sword-stick, at least a dagger-stick into the bargain. It had sprung to young master's defence. It now advanced upon the sailor, followed by Mansie. The gorilla had turned an ashen grey, as who would not in similar circumstances.

"I guess I was only kidding," he said, in a sapless voice.

"Give me back my cane!" cried Mansie. Backing away, the sailor tendered it.

But now pandemonium broke loose. Some of his shipmates rushed to the revenge, and a trusted lighting-hand threw the switch just in time. All was plunged in darkness, the music stopped, screaming and shouting were heard instead of muted harmonies. But Mansie had seen the door, and so had the cane. They made for it, with Myrtle hauling behind. In a second they were on the landing. Mansie thought that explanations would be lengthy and might with more profit be offered on another occasion. He slipped the dagger back into its malacca sheath. With it in one hand and Myrtle on the other he ran down the stairs and straight past the chocolate attendant into a waiting taxi-cab.

Disappointed as was the taxi-driver that his fare was not an American, he gruffly asked where Mansie wished to go.

"No. 2 Bleachfield, driver!" cried Mansie, happy to recall that he still had nineteen pounds in his wallet, and that he had been careful to transfer it from his own suit when he changed. He and Myrtle sank back in the rich upholstery. When he turned round to look at her, she threw her arms round his neck and pressed warm and fragrant kisses upon his lips. He surrendered to the blissful delirium. Suddenly Myrtle broke it off.

"Oh, Mansie," she breathed, "I always wanted you. You are so nice and gentle!"

She placed her head against his manly chest and lay there very still.

"What! I nice and gentle?" thought Mansie, with the merest trace of indignation. "I who have threatened an American sailor with a knife? I suppose she still thinks I am Magnus Thin. If I am Magnus Kincaid, I am probably something of a desperado and she would probably do well to get out and walk. But I do not think even Thin would be such a fool as to suggest that."

CHAPTER
ELEVEN

Mrs Thin's Confession

Mansie stood long on the stairs whispering with Myrtle. Everything they said to one another seemed beautiful, mysterious, secret, sweet and unforgettable. The street door opened, a tired little foot was heard on the stone steps, and Mrs Thin passed them, so close that they might have reached out and touched her. She looked neither to right nor to left, but climbed up to the top landing. Mansie could just make out that she was carrying his coat, muffler and cap. Then Ned Turpin came in. When he saw who was standing at the angle of the stair, he squirmed as if the dagger were pressed against his posterior, and gave them the widest possible berth. Soon after, with many undertakings that they would see one another at the soonest, they parted and vanished regretfully, held up by last kisses and hand-clasps, through their respective portals. The light was out in his mother's room, for which Mansie felt thankful. He crept off to bed, placed the cane against the wall and, having had a strenuous evening, slept like a top.

In the morning it was evident that Mrs Thin had resolved not to refer to the events of the night before. His overcoat hung as usual in the lobby, where he always placed it on return from work.

"We are a little later for breakfast than usual," she said as she ladled out the porridge, "but last night I accepted a professional engagement of an unusual nature and a little beyond my usual scope. I was deputising for Mrs Dooley in the cloakroom of a place of entertainment. While it is not my habit to criticise my employers, I cannot refrain from wondering why the police have not yet intervened."

"Is that the Osiris?" said Mansie. "I know it."

He was thinking to himself, it is all very well for mother to act as if nothing had happened. Methinks that confesses her guilt, for had my case been weaker than hers, no doubt we should have had it exposed and dissected on a cold slab. But explanations can scarcely be avoided. Yet breakfast is neither the place nor the time. I shall leave them till after high tea.

"Do you want to hear the weather forecast?" asked his mother, in a beguiling tone.

"No, thank you," said Mansie. "I have so much to think of that is simply not affected by the state of the weather that I shall give it a miss."

He rose and left the table. At the Jupiter Assurance Office he was somewhat late, for the first time in his career, but that did not trouble him. He had scarcely seated himself at his desk when a boy came round with the message, "Mr Woodburn wishes to see you." These words might once have filled him with dire speculation. Now he advanced to the presence with jaunty step.

Mr Woodburn had taken up a strong defensive position behind the broad acres of his desk, on which he had also thrown up paper-works that might have daunted the bravest.

"Sit down, Thin," he said genially, despite a certain pale and thoughtful cast upon his face. "I have been meaning to speak to you. I have been keeping a close eye on your work for some time past. It has been improving vastly and giving me great personal satisfaction, particularly as — if I may remind you — you are to some extent a private discovery of my own, and you may be said to owe your entire career to me. I think that the time has come to offer you well-merited promotion. I am happy to say that a vacancy has occurred for a new manager for the John o' Groats branch. My boy, it is yours! Let me be the first to congratulate you upon this great step forward."

He rose and leaned with outstretched hand across the top of his desk.

"John o' Groats!" thought Mansie in alarm. "I will never see Myrtle more!" He spurned the managerial paw.

"What?" exclaimed Mr Woodburn. "You decline this unique opportunity? Have you thought of the advantages? The salary goes twice as far in these country places, where one may supplement the rations by scraping shell-fish from the rocks, robbing the nests of wild birds, and catching saithe from the jetty."

"I do not intend to leave Edinburgh," said Mansie with great obstinacy.

Mr Woodburn sat back in his chair and made the best of a bad job.

"I feared as much," he said. "You win, Thin! Very well, the post of deputy supervisor of the claims department is yours. It places you on the high road to the

136

summit. Do not ask me for more. And I shall put you up for membership of my club. We must stick together, my dear boy, that is the first lesson to be learned."

Armed with this good news, Mansie left the room. The cane, he felt, had done it again.

But as he sat at his desk, apparently industrious, his thoughts were not upon promotion, or life assurance, or even Myrtle. He was more obsessed than ever before by this question of his own parentage, and which were the impulses that in the end would impetuously take command of his being. A blank sheet of scribbling paper lay before him. He divided it in two with a pencil line, writing "Thin" at the head of one half, "Kincaid" at the head of the other. Under "Thin" he then wrote, "fraud," "no corporeal existence," "too good to be true." Yet even as he wrote, he seemed to see the look of gentle reproach in the eyes of the first mate as he was about to be engulfed. Really it was too much! This fellow, who was less than a dream or fantasy, kept interfering with his mute appeal. He turned to "Kincaid" and there found a plethora of evidence. He wrote down in quick succession "thrombosis," "theatre," "Border Widow's Lament," "organ music," "Madame Désirée," "others?" "Italian cathedrals". He was beginning to have a picture of old Kincaid, yet hazily as through a haar. He saw him as elderly, a stout little roué, walking along with many a swing and lunge of the malacca cane. For some reason, probably the "Border Widow's Lament," he had a complexion of cayenne, which was reflected in the ruddy tan of his well-polished shoes. He wore a brown suit of good cut, and a canary waistcoat with brass

137

buttons. His flat was a bachelor one, and he was cared for by a silent manservant. He visited his ladies in the afternoon. Although one might not guess it at a glance, his constitution was Herculean. When others slipped under the table, he remained grinning in his chair. In the morning he swallowed, with courage, the pick-me-up that caused the bravest of his boon companions to quail. A sinister man, yet of consummate fascination, which could draw the young in his wake as on a string. Mansie was both frightened by him and wished to make his fuller acquaintance. That, alas, was impossible. He found himself amazed by the quickness of his regret. The old man was dead! He had never known the one whose Jove-like loving had granted him this existence, which was now glorified by all the splendour of Myrtle Bremner. This full life he had led! Not perhaps according to the codes of any of the sects who poured their doctrines into Mrs Thin's ear from the spluttering fountain of the loudspeaker. Moderator, Archbishop, Chief Rabbi — not one of them would commend old man Kincaid. Yet their lives and their faces were thin and angular compared with his. Where they danced precariously on a moral tight-rope, he took the width of the road.

So he thought and doodled on the paper, as if he were working out a complex calculation. Mr Woodburn passed through the office with an ingratiating smile towards Mansie. He could not refrain from odious comparisons between the unashamed and sweeping recreations of Mr Kincaid and the petty, furtive lust in which he had surprised the general manager. What they were at could be boiled down to a similar essence in the end, yet whereas one achieved the squalid air of sin, the other reached up to the philosophic heights of hedonism.

In the evening he picked the malacca cane out of the umbrella stand and set off homeward. For some reason unknown to himself, but doubtless familiar to his magic wand, he deviated from his usual direct path and found himself passing the Gothic door of St Ninian's. The organ was pealing within, and in a flash he recalled that this was the place and the hour of Dr Plumdough's organ recital. This was indeed bewildering. Mansie could not envisage old man Kincaid in a church. Nevertheless, had he been alive, he would have slipped in to hear the thunderous manipulation of his crony Plumdough. Mansie decided to follow his example.

Mansie had never entered a church before and until last night would have panicked at the thought. But now a curiosity worthy of old Kincaid inspired him. He would take a look and listen, without committing himself.

St Ninian's was almost the only church in the city which did not disdain a frank appeal to the eye and to the ear. Not that it was the act of piety of an age of faith. On the contrary, it represented the uneasy conscience of an age devoted to Mammon, and in their erection of a temple to the Unknown God, whom they feared might win out in the end, the congregations had pursued a richness which would have been pleasing in the sight of their more familiar deity. This was, in short, not one of those bare kirks which throw the worshipper hard against his own resources; it attempted to remind them

139

they were not far from the palm court of their favourite hotel. So this is a church, thought Mansie, remembering the squalid little room with the linoleum up the walls where the Children of Gabriel used to meet. A beadle handed him a white sheet on which were written the names of various pieces of music, but as titles meant no more to Mansie than did opus numbers he stuffed it into his pocket and sat down on one of the uncomfortable grass-bottomed chairs.

For some time the music rolled round and round, like the grumblings of an electric storm in the Pentland Hills, punctuated by the bleatings of lost lambs and strayed seabirds. But no one could have listened for more than a few minutes to the playing of Dr Plumdough without feeling that he was present at a sort of creation, when the waters were separated from the dry land, the flowers and the fishes sent to their appointed place and lights set to rule both the day and the night. His digital and pedal dexterity partook of the attributes of divine certainty. Fingers ran over the keys like running brooks over the face of a cliff, because they could not help it. Themes called out like curlews high up among the Lammermuirs on a June day, and were answered by the assault of long breakers on the Bass. Larks soared, new-born lambs skipped on the hill-sides. Myrtle, bare-footed and in a blue robe, came walking through the midst of a field of corn, the next moment she had slipped through his hands like a ghost. She was dead, or so he heard in some terrible rumour which for long he could not believe. And then he lay weeping inconsolably on her grave. But the trumpets sounded, the armies marched forth. A hero's death at least remained for him. Against every omen, the unequal contest ended in victory. They were marching through the streets, while all the inhabitants laughed and threw down roses on them from the topmost windows.

A thousand lives, rich in experience, were showered upon him, and at last his mind wilted from exhaustion. Only then did he begin to be touched by the music for its own sake. It looped itself round and round him in voluptuous and never-ending curves; as Dr Plumdough pulled out fresh stops the colours changed, and yet there were no reds and blues. I know why he came here, thought Mansie, for here is the paradisal retreat of the senses. Just then the music stopped, and the audience, which was not large, began to skail. When Mansie reached the door, Dr Plumdough was there, shaking hands with a few friends. He turned to Mansie.

"Ah, dear boy, I'm glad you came! You care about the real things! What is jazz? Merely the beating of the jungle tom-toms, while the poor primitives shiver and quake under the spell. Music is not orgiastic, my dear fellow, as too many suppose. It is the tapestry that was woven by the Lady of Shallott. You think I am disappointed because to-night my music was heard by only a handful of the *cognoscenti*? Not a bit of it, my boy! You do not suppose that in this illiterate, insensitive and beastly world more could penetrate to these high delights? Excellence does not only refuse to follow numbers; it marches straight off in the contrary direction. If St Ninian's had been full to-night, I could not have slept for worry. But I could tell by your face you could claim a seat in the enchanted circle. You can leave your collection on that pewter plate."

When he reached home, Mrs Thin had the wireless on and a kipper waiting. Mansie could see that she was terrified of him, and would have liked to pretend that last night had not been. But he knew that he had reached the most painful stage of his enquiry, that which concerned his mother. He supposed she was his mother. No one should lightly pry into the story of his own birth. He wanted to know, but wished to use her with all tenderness. The old familiar gambits provided the opening to a conversation.

"These kippers appear to have lost some of the succulence of a week ago," he remarked as easily as possible.

"That is not surprising," replied Mrs Thin; "the Forth herring season is now at an end."

"Talking of the Forth," said Mansie, "I was down in the Port of Leith last night. There I met a mariner who had formed one of the ship's company of the *Fitful Head*."

Mrs Thin looked closely at her plate, but made no reply.

Mansie continued, "He told me that the *Fitful Head* is now owned by a Greek concern, the Corinth and Patmos Shipping Company I think he called it. So far as I can understand, it never foundered on the Pentland Skerries at all."

Mrs Thin tried the bold front.

"Who ought to know that?" she demanded. "Some lying tar or the widow of the first mate."

"According to my information, the *Fitful Head* never had a first mate of the name of Magnus Thin. She was never commanded by a master of the name of Copinsay. Mother, the whole thing was a fairy tale, and you must be aware of that fact. If you had provided me with a family tree stretching back to the Norman Conquest, you could not have taken me further in."

Mrs Thin burst into tears.

"I did it for the best!" she wailed. "I have always striven to do my duty. And what happens at the end of the day? I earn the repute of impostor and common liar!"

Mansie was moved with deep but inarticulate compassion. He rose and stood behind her chair, patting her shoulders and sometimes kissing her grey hair.

"It was all for your sake. I wanted you to have a proper life. You will never believe me now, but I am a respectable woman. It is the one thing I have always wanted to be since you were born — respectable!"

"Surely it would have been respectable to tell me the truth," he gently suggested.

"That's all you know! You always were a simple child! That's why I was so afraid for you," she sobbed.

"Calm down, mother, and tell me what happened," he said. She heaved more regularly, like the sea after a great storm, until only a slight ground-swell remained.

"Little did I think that these lips would ever utter the story of my shame to mortal man, let alone to the child of my body," she began, being like all elderly Scotswomen a finished stylist. "You will excuse me if I do not look you in the eye. But I could not bear it. There

143

are some things that may be said only by looking hard at the jam dish."

Mansie gave his willing and softly-spoken assent.

His mother half-turned away from him and began her confession.

"I was," she said, "a simple country girl, and those who know only modern children cannot comprehend how simple country girls could be in the days of my youth. Modern parents, if I may judge by the Chisholms, snatch their offspring at the earliest possible moment from the age of innocence. They do not guard their talk before them, in fact they are, like sailors in the fo'castle of a windjammer, unnecessarily outspoken. They flaunt their ugly, grown-up bodies before them, and drum into their little pink ears the beastliness of human life. How differently was I reared on the far island where I was born! There were mermaids in the sea, waiting to beguile young fishermen, and the seal people came to rest on the rocks underneath the headland. I myself have lain watching them there with Magnus, and nearly understood their talk."

"With Magnus?" Mansie could not repress the interruption.

"I am coming to him," said Mrs Thin, "in a moment. I must tell you some day about the seal people, for it was through them that I suffered my first bitter loss. I had a dear elder sister named Sunniva. One day when she was eighteen a great silkie came ashore and stole her away. My mother died shortly afterwards, nor did my father Goodlad Thin ever quite recover from the blow."

"Then your name was Thin!" cried Mansie.

"Yes, yes, I fear so. I could not give you any name but my own. Goodlad Thin was a fisherman and a patriarch. According to the season he anchored his creels in the bay, sailed far out into the Atlantic after cod or worked on the croft on the brow of the hill. We had sheep with blue and copper fleeces, a little heifer that had survived the evil eye of our witch, and our ponies ran wild on the scathold above."

"Go on!" cried Mansie, scarcely able to contain himself.

"As I remember my childhood, it was always sunshine and wind. There were no woebegone half-and-half days as there are now. I do not say we never had bad weather. But if it was, we children were excited and wild. The rain wetted the thatch and softened the earthen floor, it washed the mud from the chinks of the unmortared stone wall. Great gales strove to wrench our little house from the slab of lava on which it was built, and father alone was strong enough to venture out of doors and to weight down the house with more and more great boulders. The cow would go dry, and the hens leave off laying. We had nothing to eat but moistened handfuls of oatmeal. We would sit tending the peat, drying the rain-soaked turves by the hot ash of the losing fire. Thor and Odin were wrestling outside, and we had to crouch low lest we should be ground under their heels."

Mansie felt that his mother was wandering from the point. "But Mansie?" he reminded her.

A look of young fondness such as he had never seen except in Myrtle's eyes shone out at the jam dish.

"Ah, Mansie — he was the boy on the next croft. I could not remember when I knew him first, for we were ages and grew up together. No, we only began to grow up. We were always out in the sun and the wind. He was not above playing in my house of broken dishes at the end of the peatstack, and I was standing on the shore of the loch when he caught his first sea-trout on a borrowed line. As he grew older he went to the deep sea in my father's yawl, for Goodlad Thin had no son and thought much of Magnus.

"One day we were lying on the headland listening to the seals and trying to understand their tongue, which is so like that of the human race that one could swear that the full meaning might have been caught if only one had heard a little better, when the seals all dived under the sea. We looked up and saw that the mail-steamer with its snow-white bridge and primrose funnels was passing by. Mansie — yes, that is what I called him — Mansie stared long at it. He smiled to himself and a cold hand gripped my heart, Once I would have watched the steamer too. But now I saw only him. 'What will you do when you grow big?' I asked. He never took his eyes off the mail-steamer. 'I shall be a mate on a ship like that,' he said. Then I began to cry without noise and it was long before he saw me. When he did, he laughed so kindly and took my hand. 'Never fear,' he told me then, 'I shall take you with me. We shall have a house in Aberdeen or Edinburgh like Uncle Laurence, and I shall always come there between voyages.'

"From that moment all seemed settled, and time moved forward with a lengthened stride. Uncle Laurence was to send Mansie to the nautical college. In the meanwhile he sailed everywhere with my father.

Already my heart leapt like a young wife's when I heard the luderhorn from the returning yawl blown across the firth to warn us of their coming. I would run down to the shore to welcome my father's yawl, but it was not my father I ran to welcome, or with thoughts for him in my heart that I helped to haul their boat safely into the noost.

"It was then that my father began to go mad. He was forever brooding on the lost Sunniva who had run off with the silkie. He would stalk the seals along the shore in the hope that she might be there, sunning herself in their company. Although she was never there, his hopes grew stronger. Once he was certain that she slipped off the rock under a great wave as he leaned over the cliff. This madness was the end of him, and of my Mansie too."

Mrs Thin paused for a long time, and the clock ticked louder.

"They were far out in the deep, fishing with the other yawls, when my father saw two seals in company swimming to the westward. 'Take up the lines!' he shouted. 'There she swims, with the silkie by her side!' What Mansie thought, I do not know, or the other men in the yawl, but they drew up their lines and trimmed the sail, and soon were out of sight across the horizon. That night the great storm blew up. The rest of the fleet made the firth of home in safety, but my father's yawl, and those in it, were never seen again."

Mansie was listening to her story like a child, but could not see what it had to do with him. His mother began to speak again, but rapidly.

Do not ask me to tell you all of the next part of my story. The animals go out on to the hill-side, and the

147

human kind must hide themselves too. I was distracted with grief and left all alone. The croft was sold and the gear, but there was little money forthcoming and it scarcely paid my fare on the mail-steamer. When I came to the town I took service, in the house of that man whom I know you have discovered to be your father. That was his house, where you went last night. He called me his wild sea-pink, and I lost my will whenever he looked at me."

My wild sea-pink! Mansie started at the metaphor, which his mother repeated with a certain defiant pride. He was covered with confusion and embarrassment.

"He was a horrible man. He left me with shame after pleasure. Mansie could never have done that, because he had a loving nature. The other was Magnus too, but he had no love, no heart that I could touch. When he threw me away and you were born, I vowed that you should never learn of such an evil man. So I brought Mansie to life to be your father."

His mother suddenly looked up at Mansie and smiled.

"I think I have succeeded," she said. "I think you are more of Mansie Thin than Magnus Kincaid!"

CHAPTER
TWELVE

The Quest Pursued

Although he had begun to suspect that some such confession of indiscretion in youth must be in store for him, Mansie was unprepared for the circumstances with which Mrs Thin had decked out her acknowledgment. He was a good son, and his first feelings were of indignation and wrath against his mother's betrayer. The vile, voluptuous cynic, thus to deceive and then to abandon his uprooted sea-pink, so soon to wither into the aged domestic help whom he had known all his life! By now he had such a strong impression of the continuing existence of old Kincaid that he almost picked up the cane and went in search of him. Only by an effort of reason did he convince himself that Kincaid was as dead as Magnus Thin. An uneasy thought ran through his mind. Were they truly dead, or only unassailable?

Mrs Thin repeatedly tried to justify her imposture to him in the name of respectability. "I wanted you to have a respectable home, a respectable history and respectable thoughts," she said piteously. "If I had not told you lies, you might have thought me a loose woman. I was no looser than any other woman — only innocent, at a disadvantage and swept away. I had to find someone to be an example to you."

But what was respectability? Only the disguise under which life tried to hide its passionate and astonishing face. Life with its trembling lip, always afraid to look other men in the eye, for fear of their scorn and their jibes. Yet respectability was more, thought Mansie. It was the intense desire of sufferers not to pass on their disease, but to see their children ride on calm, untroubled waters. It was a conspiracy that pain, poverty and evil had never yet invaded the little Eden of the family. But fate had doomed it to be broken in the end.

Of all the tricks which were being played upon Mansie, one of the most curious was the growing clarity of Magnus Thin, both as boy and as first mate. As the cayenne countenance of Kincaid shone with a darker glow before his mind, so on the other side he could see the clear sailor's eyes of Thin fixed upon him with an unwinking and unwavering stare. He hung there like the serene effigy of a saint whose legend has been blown upon but who does not seem to care. Mrs Thin had indeed erected him into a spiritual father for her son. Yet as the days passed, Mansie began to kick against his infallible sweetness, his blamelessness and his silence. For even when Mansie could see him most clearly in his mind's eye, he never allowed his lips to move.

On the other hand, the more he resented the father of his flesh, the stronger grew the spell which old Kincaid had begun to exercise over him ever since the night when his malacca cane reached him by such devious and second-hand ways. For enjoying then discarding his mother, Mansie would never forgive him. But his absorption in him grew, by the working of fatalism. He

150

wanted to fathom the secrets of his own nature, and only one line of investigation was possible. I inherit from Kincaid, and not from Thin, he told himself. The blood of that gross sensualist, that cynic, that user of other souls boils through my veins. The most I could ever have from Thin is a veneer, a fraction of an inch thick.

And after all, he told himself, he was already indebted to Kincaid for a great deal. He did not mean his twenty pounds, or his undeserved promotion at the office, or even Myrtle — all gifts which could be traced directly or indirectly to the activities of the cane. No, he had only to compare his life before and after his journey along the Street of a Thousand Bargains. Before that day he had been a wizened little thing, like a seed that has shrivelled away from the moisture, air and light; he had been governed by superimposed routines; his only lighter interest had been the insignificant vagaries of the Scottish climate; he had made a foolish victim for quacks who talked with certainty of what is hid from the eyes of man, and had walked in terror of catastrophes in which the disappearance of such a sluggish lizard as himself could not conceivably be treated as of any importance. But since that day he had been stuffed full of unaccountable adventures, sudden somersaults of fortune and unearned rewards. He had tasted champagne, organ music, the dance, the lips of the remote and unapproachable beauty on the floor below. Ned Turpin stood out of his way, and the neighbours whispered in awestruck tones as he strolled past.

Most unexpectedly, his behaviour towards Myrtle began to change. He had regarded her as a little haloed goddess, who smiled upon him by her favour, an immortal condescension beyond the wit of man. Now when he said good-night in the small hours at the bend of the stair he fiercely tugged her hair, bit the lobes of her ear and used her so cruelly that she cried. Yet she loved him more and could deny him nothing, although in the morning she seemed pale and afraid.

They often went back to the Osiris, where the appearance of Mansie with his cane in one hand and his girl on the other arm caused a momentary hush every time he entered the crowded ballroom. The rumour had gone round that with this weapon he had vanquished the entire American navy, and as the cruiser had long since sailed from the Forth there was no one to dispute the legend, which the outfaced and penurious natives longed in their hearts to believe. Madame Désirée made much of him. The old procuress, her days of omnidirectional love in her own person at last at an end, delighted to remind herself of her heyday by helping on the love-making of others. She smiled upon them continually, and placed one of the private supper-rooms perpetually at their service.

And this was old Kincaid's mansion. Mansie began to feel as if he had inherited that too. Madame Désirée could tell him how it had been arranged in the days before he gave it up for the more central flat in the West End — where the library had been, where the music-room, where the dining-room, hung with the choicest paintings of Peploe, Cadell and Leslie Hunter, where the great bedroom adorned with amoretti. This private supper-room had once been the dressing-room where he kept his clothes and a cupboard full of whiskies and brandies.

One night he was sitting alone in the room. Myrtle had been claimed for a dance by one of the acquaintances they had made here. He had been unwilling to let her go at first, but consented in the end, for the wine had made him indolent and tolerant. Through the wall the rhythm of the dance was beating. He rose and turned off all the lights except one shaded table-lamp. He closed his eyes and leaned back comfortably in the elbow-chair. Without knowing it, he was half-awake, half in a dose.

That was when he heard a deep, laughing voice say over his shoulder, "My boy!" The voice, though deep, was soft and conspiratorial, like a naughty boy's about to suggest some prank under the very nose of authority. Mansie did not have to ask whose voice it was. There could be no other such. He tried to turn, but a cramp seemed to have seized him. He could not shift in his chair, or even move his neck.

"My boy!" said the voice. "I like you. More, I'm proud of you. I'm watching your progress with great interest — would it surprise you if I said with vast approval? My seed was like the thistle's. It blew on every wind, and I cared not if it sprouted, but now that I happen upon this sturdy and promising plant I am gratified. I had no faith in plan, foresight or consideration, and see how splendidly justified I am in you. I cast you adrift, but in good time my legacy fell into your hands and see how you are using it! You have reproached me, I know! I am glad! What man of spirit would not! But you cannot escape me in the end. Do not

153

waste pity and tears on that simple woman who was my intermediary in the business. She was one of those flowers that bloom once, then return to a crop of dull and unappetising foliage. She was born to be a martyr, to make the most of little, and to keep a brave face to the world. She has been happiest in the exercise of these pitiable virtues. I gave her moments beyond her scope, which could never have extended to that grasp of this earthly life which belongs to you, my boy, and to me."

Mansie made a superhuman effort to swivel his head upon his shoulders, but all power had ebbed from his muscles.

"My ghost knows only one regret," the voice continued. "It is that you and I should not have enjoyed a carouse together. You have been seeking an answer to the riddles of your sphinx-like nature. Ah, my boy, that is the great trick of creation by which mortals are eternally teased. It is within their power to see clearly through every fog but that one. Yet it can be penetrated. Oh yes, I assure you! I think I can say that I know the drill. If only you and I could contrive to meet —"

His voice trailed off in an infinitude of possibility. There was a pause in which Mansie pondered all that had been said.

"You see," the spirit of old Kincaid continued in his most persuasive manner, "I possess the key of knowledge, and I should be happy, very happy indeed, to pass it on to you. If only we could meet — couldn't you and I fix up a date together?"

Mansie found his muscular control sufficiently to nod.

"Ah, splendid! The desire is mutual!" the voice exclaimed with cordiality. "What could be more auspicious? Let me look at my dates — Ah yes, to-morrow night, how would to-morrow night suit?"

"Very well," breathed Mansie.

"Then I'll jot it down. To-morrow night — *D'accord!* But of course there's one thing we must bear in mind. The crowd. I'm not very good with people nowadays. And what a bunch they are! Really! Just the sort of riff-raff with whom old Désirée feels thoroughly at home! But a little too much, don't you think? Especially since you and I want to get down to cases, without other people butting in. For instance, that wench of yours, rather charming — though I shouldn't take it quite so seriously, my dear fellow, if a much older sinner may speak — she would be a little *de trop*, don't you agree? She'll be back in a moment and I'm afraid I'll have to clear out."

Mansie was making superhuman efforts to move.

"No, we don't want the common herd buzzing about all over the place, like wasps when you're having tea at Lochearnhead. We'll give them a chance to scatter to the four winds, don't you think? So let us say here, in this spot, to-morrow night, after they've cleared out. We'll have a little dinner together. My boy, I think I can promise you a dinner you'll remember."

He had scarcely uttered these words when Mansie broke the enchantment which had seized his limbs. As he turned his head, he was able to catch a vanishing glimpse of the cayenne countenance he knew so well without an introduction. Then all went black.

Mansie had passed out. That is admitted to be a disgraceful way to behave, but at least it is better than passing on. The state was also one with which the Osiris was competent to deal, being regularly in practice. When Myrtle returned to the supper-room she found her sweetheart listless in his chair like a sack of potatoes. The state was new to her, but his heavy breathing consoled her that he was still alive. She pressed him, cajoled him and shook him, but all in vain. By a stroke of good luck Madame Désirée looked in, on one of her tours of inspection. The symptoms were familiar.

"Let him snore, girl!" she said. "Then cart him home!"

Myrtle was a good girl, by no means the flighty minx for which she was being written down in the Bleachfield district, She had but one ambition, which was none the less real for never being stated. She looked confidently to the day when she would leave the shop where she worked, marry, settle down and reign over a small family like a primitive queen. She had singled out Mansie as the man who might be the keystone of the arch of her design. He had seemed to her the ideal of steadiness.

Now as she sat and listened to his snores, she was worried. There was a hostile influence which she could not understand, and not far away at that. It had reached its pinnacle in this room, but often of late she had felt it reaching out after him and even possessing him. At these times she was afraid. The boy whose arm she liked to feel round her waist seemed strange, unknown and terrifying. Yes, there was an unseen enemy which she had to fight. As she could not see where the enemy lurked, there was only one course open to her, and that was to stand sentinel over his soul.

Half an hour later Mansie awoke. He was amenable to reason, and followed her quietly into the waiting taxi-cab. But he did not seem certain where he was or what he was doing. He babbled of the strange appointment he had made when she was absent and of the cayenne face at his shoulder.

Myrtle was not only a good girl; she was practical and hard-headed. She might easily have dismissed his ramblings as a by-product of the mixing of drinks which had evidently taken place. But she knew when she was at grips with the enemy. As she snuggled close to Mansie in the back of the cab, she was as alert as a beautiful spy before whom the young subaltern tumbles out his country's secrets.

CHAPTER
THIRTEEN

Dinner with the Dead

Next morning Mansie saw the world in a greenish light. He bit his mother's nose off at breakfast. At the office he was sour and unfriendly. He and Myrtle always met for lunch in the milk-bar, where, huddled together over a shake and sandwich, they enjoyed perfect bliss. Now he barely grunted out his order, then sat with his brow on the palm of his hand. Who does not envy those Arcadians who achieve happiness the lactic way? Alas, Mansie was no longer of their number. In vain did Myrtle press his knee and ask, "What's the matter, sweetie?" He merely removed the hand he would once have pressed close. Myrtle felt the palisade go up about him. She was even more frightened in broad daylight than she had been in the supper-room with its sinfully shaded lamps.

Once or twice Mansie felt the pang that passes through every man when he sees love, beauty, simplicity at his feet and yet turns away to find — what? That is the worst of allowing oneself to be eaten up by a quest, that vista down the side roads where one may not linger. Mansie was wistfully aware of some grievous folly that had captured him, yet unable to draw back. After to-night it

158

might be different. But the appointment with the dead had to be kept.

Mansie told Myrtle that he needed a quiet night and intended to have it. He felt, he said, that he had been going his dinger; it was time to call a halt herself. For herself, he thought that she was looking a little tired, and that sleep would restore the roses. Myrtle knew by the light of nature that something is amiss when a lover notices that his loved one is tired.

He told his mother much the same story. There was, of course, no need to hurry, for the Osiris was to be the place of meeting and it would not be empty till after midnight. He would pretend to read, then steal out into the night when his mother was asleep. He reckoned that if he left home by midnight, he would be in excellent time.

Yawning ostentatiously, he retired to his room and put out the light. There was no point in undressing, but he sat down in his armchair to rest. He glanced once or twice at his watch with the luminous dial. The minutes seemed reluctant to move forward at his pace. He would wait for five minutes and then find the hands of his watch registered only one. The springs of Mrs Thin's bed twanged once or twice in the next room, and the pulley squeaked in the flat below.

He must have fallen into a light doze, for he awoke suddenly, cramped with cold. The moon was shining with diamond clarity, as if there were a touch of frost in the air, and lighting up the handle of the malacca cane where he had thrown it on the bed. He glanced quickly at his watch. It read two minutes after twelve. Good heavens, he thought, I shall be late, and if there is one fault I cannot abide it is being late for appointments.

How he took the next step was not clear to Manise, indeed many steps of that unpredictable night remained shrouded in a mist forever afterwards. But he smoothed his hair, silently lifted the window at the sash, picked up the malacca cane and stood up on the ledge high up on the Bleachfield tenement. He lacked fear; he had also the most delicious sensation of lacking weight. The slates of a garage in a back lane were glittering with sequins of frost. Two wild duck flew from the airt of the Pentlands, following the course of the Water of Leith as if they were the pilots of human aircraft, and quacking now and then in a short staccato way. An owl flew across his face in the direction of the Botanic Garden.

Grasping the cane, which became a kind of joy-stick, he took off confidently from the window-ledge and headed straight for Murrayfield with a dreamy, undulating motion, which brought him now quite close to the roof-tops, then high above them. The Water of Leith rolled out the moonlight into a ribbon of quicksilver. He followed it steadily through Stockbridge and the Dean Village, sometimes peeping in at one of the rare lighted windows to see whether it contained a sick-bed or a ceilidh. The Osiris — or Kincaid Towers, as he now preferred to think of it — presented an unfamiliar shape to birds, but he found it without much difficulty and made a cushiony landing on the drive in front of the portico, just as if he were coming down on a very luxurious down-quilt. He fell right over on his back, but soon picked himself up, went through the motions of dusting himself (for there was no dust upon him) and advanced towards the door. The door was closed, but when a door is closed the most natural course is to ring. Mansie did so.

He had not long to wait. A light came on behind the fanlight, a silvery light, unlike the golden gleam which welcomed visitors to the dance club, and the door was opened by a black servant in a crimson turban, with a jewel and egret's feather in the middle of his forehead. He looked remarkably like a conjurer's assistant, indeed Mansie recalled having seen him before, probably in a music-hall. He bowed to the earth and murmured, "Sahib?"

"I have called to see Señor Kincaid," said Mansie sharply. He was surprised to hear that Kincaid was a señor, but he did not seem to be in full control either of his movements or of his utterances, and after all the title seemed remarkably appropriate.

The oriental servant said "Follow!" with an imperious gesture. Drawing three Indian clubs from the recesses of his pantaloons, he swung them into the air and kept them spinning as easily as if they were celluloid balls on a waterjet at a fair-ground. With a nonchalant step he strolled along the passage, Mansie following behind.

They were in the Osiris, yet it was not the Osiris. The Oriental was so much occupied by his trick that he walked quite slowly, giving Mansie plenty of time to inspect the big game trophies, suits of armour and ancient weapons that hung from the wall and stood in every corner. On the floor were leopard, bear, tiger and lion skins. There were pikes, saracens' scimitars, flint-

161

lock pistols, old fowling-pieces, a Highland claymore, the rapier which killed its man in the last duel fought in Scotland and a cat-o'-nine-tails.

The Oriental led the way upstairs. The steps were bare of waxed pine, but on the floor above Persian rugs of the most exquisite pattern and tread lay underfoot. Here there was no adornment on the walls except a number of elegant pictures by Watteau and Fragonard. A fragrance that transformed breathing into one of the highest and subtlest pleasures hung in the air. Just then they came to the doors of the ballroom, which seemed to open of their own accord but were no doubt manipulated by the two footmen whom Mansie could see standing inside, in dark green liveries with silver facings. The Oriental threw a rope into the air, climbed up it and vanished. A major-domo came forward, in a more splendiferous version of the livery worn by the footmen and bearing a vast mace such as drum-majors carry. He tossed it in the air and chanted:

"Way for the most noble and right honourable Magnus Thin-Kincaid, hereditary standard-bearer for the human race and Bleachfield Pursuivant, Insurant Extraordinary and helluva nice guy!"

The major-domo was now seen to be the American sailor. He began to chew gum and walked away. Mansie heard the clapping of hands like water falling at the far end of a cavern and advanced into the room. Without being told, he knew this to be the dining-room and looked round for the valuable pictures which Madame Désirée had told him used to be there. But the lighting was bad; a mouse-like mist hung over everything, and vision stopped short before the limits of the room were reached.

Yet he could see clearly enough to discern at the top of the room a long high table arranged in an arc. It was draped in white damask and covered with cutlery and crystal dishes. Raised up on a dais at the centre of the table was old Kincaid, with Madame Désirée on his right. They were leaning forward and peering at him, with amused yet greedy eyes. Mademoiselle Julie was there, and Alois and the healthy barman got up in a pink coat. What greatly surprised Mansie was to recognise Brothers Jeroboam, Methuselah and Gamaliel, who was cuddling Sister Dinah at the bottom right-hand corner of the table. Brother Methuselah wore the same detached smile as ever, but Brother Jeroboam was leaning forward on the white cloth with his nostrils back. Mansie felt without resentment towards the Children, even glad to see them again.

Old Kincaid spoke in his low-pitched voice.

"Sit down, my boy!" he said, and indicated a little table set separately. Mansie sat and found that it was very low. Old Kincaid and his guests were all at a higher level and seemed to be grinning down at him from all directions.

"There's not much can be done on an empty stomach — and without a dinkie, a teeny-weeny dinkie," he observed quite jocularly. Then without warning he flew off into a violent temper.

"Demme!" he shouted. "Where's Turpin? What does he do with my champagne? Pour it down his own gullet?

That man's a twister and a thief! Turpin, demme, Turpin, where are you?"

Turpin appeared behind Kincaid's chair, trembling with fright.

"Here, sir! Here, Mr Kincaid!" he whimpered.

For answer old Kincaid swivelled in his chair and with a sharp jerk (such was his stupendous strength) knocked Turpin off his feet. He kicked him and cuffed him till the great dining-room pulsated with his ululations. Then with as swift a change again, old Kincaid desisted and turned a friendly smile on Mansie.

"That's the only way to treat a rogue," he remarked. "The fellow's a bully, of course, and bullying is the only language he understands. My dear boy, I want you to appreciate the meanness and squalor of all his kind. They're always cowards. Don't pity them! That's the mark of a soft head."

Mansie was glad of the reminder, for he had been on the point of leaping to his feet to remonstrate with old Kincaid as he savagely kicked Turpin in the ribs, but somehow the power seemed to have gone out of his legs. He was bound to admit that Turpin seemed none the worse when he presently returned bearing a magnum of champagne. He performed a few simpering caracoles in front of Kincaid, like a whipped collie trying to curry favour, and then set off round the guests pouring a glass for each. When he came last to Mansie, his obsequiousness was almost obscene. He poured out the champagne with excessive care, often wiping the mouth of the bottle with a folded napkin, but after he had passed on, Mansie was puzzled to observe that his glass seemed empty. He peered at the glasses of those on the high table. They were a little too far away to be clearly seen; besides, the light was not good. But all the members of the company were pledging one another, throwing back bumpers and demanding re-fills. Sister Dinah was already a little tiddly. For a moment Mansie wondered if Turpin had dared to play a joke on him, but he decided against that hypothesis, for he had only to breathe the word and Turpin would be half murdered. He decided that the most polite course for a guest was to say nothing.

Dancing girls now trooped in bearing ashets with enormous oven-like silver covers, such as he had often seen cluttering the windows of the second-hand shops. They circled the tables, then simultaneously laid down their burdens with well-drilled cohesion. Mansie sniffed in anticipation but could smell nothing. Perhaps I have caught one of these confounded colds, he told himself, although I could smell the perfume on the stairs all right. Old Kincaid pinched one of the dancing girls on the behind so that she let out a delighted squeal. All the other guests laughed and applauded. Then he waved the dancing girls away. Now for the eats, thought Mansie with pleasure, for his solo flight through the frosty atmosphere had put an edge on his appetite.

But not yet. Old Kincaid held up a hand for silence. Sister Dinah was giggling so much that at first she did not heed, but the señor kept regarding her steadily until at last she too fell silent.

"I will now call upon Brother Jeroboam to offer up thanks before meat," he said with suitable gravity.

165

Brother Jeroboam laid down his glass, wiped his mouth with his napkin and closed his eyes, saying:

"Temper the flame beneath the gridiron, O mighty prince of grills and ovens, blow gently with thy infernal breath upon joints and gigots, sow fire in spices that with the wines of burning lands we may strive to assuage the thirst there from accruing, nurse, as it were lava outpoured, the omelette, the soufflé, all sauces, whether spirituous or peppered. Advance the cause of gourmandise in all lands, and place thy merciless curse upon all simple dishes, such as porridge, syrup sponge, tapioca, and other brutish concoctions we now name in our hearts. Sulphurously consume all temperance hotels, milkbars, station buffets and factory canteens, and visit with thy formidable wrath, we beseech thee, all fish-and-chip shops, starch-purveying tearooms and ice-cream saloons. And for this banquet, mighty prince of the belly and president over the lower centres, we offer up humble thanks."

The company had remained transfixed in reverent attitudes. They now relaxed gladly, as always after the formalities are behind. Mr Kincaid beamed round the table.

"I can't stand these long extempore Scotch graces," he exclaimed. "Brother Jeroboam, you must learn something shorter for the next time we meet. Let us fall to!"

He snapped his fingers. The dancing girls immediately advanced, one behind each chair, lifted the covers and began to pile food on each diner's plate.

Mansie's attention was distracted because at that moment Kincaid pointed to the opposite side of the room and called, "Are you all set, dear boy?"

166

"All set!" came the twittering voice of the Mus.Doc. "I thought some Chopin nocturnes might go with the fish, and a Beethoven sonata with the meat. And I can thoroughly recommend a dry later Fauré with the bird!"

"Excellent! Serve it up!" called old Kincaid, and almost before Mansie could look round, the piano was heard, played with a supernatural delicacy of touch. The melodies sang out and the cadenzas tumbled like rills. There was no noise of the hammers. Just behind his back Mansie saw a sleek black concert grand, which he had failed to observe before. Dr Plumdough was seated at the keyboard, more transparent than ever. His face expressed the rapture of the mood and he swept the keys with extravagant gestures. Kincaid was watching Mansie with close attention.

"I will tell you how to use those great spirits, my boy," he said in a flattering, confidential way. "It is quite simple. Make them your servants! Don't be overawed by them! Let them fetch and carry for you, let them minister unto you! And if you possess a sense of irony, your pleasure is sharpened, for you may think of all their years of discipline and desire as having one object — your own gratification. Tomates farcies! Try a fish kebab, you moth-eaten Delilah!"

He had suddenly remembered that he was neglecting Madame Désirée and now began to ladle food on to her plate with the utmost gallantry. Again, as with the wine, Mansie could not perceive any food as he knew it, but the other guests did not seem to be experiencing the same difficulty. Madame Désirée was laughing and

167

pushing away his arm from her plate, with a reiterated, *"Non, non, c'est trop!"* Brother Jeroboam had his napkin tucked into his collar and was making a pig of himself, as if he knew it would be long before he sat down to such another spread. Nor was Brother Methuselah wasting time, although he ate with more method and self-control. He did not have to spend so much time wiping his mouth and shirt-front as did Brother Jeroboam. As for Brother Gamaliel and Sister Dinah, they were like children at a treat. "Try this!" they would cry. "Ooh! how scrumptious!" And they would push spoonfuls of food down each other's throats, so that they almost choked. The habits of the others were of equal interest. Mademoiselle Julie ate in a languorous, leisurely fashion, frequently pausing to pick her teeth and to stare at the other diners. There was a slight fracas when it was discovered that Ned Turpin had crawled under the table and was pawing her legs, but she bore those physical familiarities with a wonderful indifference, even suggesting that the indecent behaviour of Turpin should be accepted as a kind of compliment. Of course, Kincaid sent Turpin about his business. The old man was not eating much himself; his chief care seemed to be for his guests.

"Turpin, you great booby, take a glass of champagne across to Dr Plumdough!" he would bark as he recognised the end of a piece. Then he would lean across the table to Mansie and say, "My boy, what's the matter with your appetite? You're making nothing of your food! Not still wasting thoughts over that common little shop-girl? Tuck in, tuck in! You cannot break the heart of a well-fed man. All women come alike to him!"

Mansie was in an awkward position. He pretended to fall to, and to his great relief old Kincaid seemed satisfied, returning to his own plate and murmuring, "Ah, we'll make a trencher-man of you yet!"

The apparatus of the meal was more elaborate than anything Mansie had ever experienced before. Finger-bowls were brought in and borne away, there were pauses when the guests lit black Russian cigarettes. Every now and then Kincaid made a fuss over some dish. The chef was called, a greasy man in a tall white hat, and there were endless tastings and explanations. During one of these Mademoiselle Julie grew bored. Rising from her place, she performed a Spanish dance quite close to Mansie's table, whispering with her castanets in his ear, and then sat down again. But before she sat down, he felt himself reaching out to touch her, just as Turpin had done. Turpin and I are not so unlike after all, he told himself, and looked up to find the cayenne visage of old *pére* Kincaid grinning at him. "All in good time!" he laughed. "You're a man, and everything is yours — all in good time!" Madame Désirée leaned over and whispered to Julie, who as usual said neither yea nor nay. She seemed a young woman without marked preferences but willing to accept instructions.

The meal was now approaching its conclusion.

"We shall soon be able to get down to serious business!" cried old Kincaid, with a roguish gesture which Mansie did not know whether to interpret by reference to an empty glass or to Mademoiselle Julie, who sat a little beyond it. Coffee was brought in by the slaves, and Turpin staggered out of the gloom under the weight of the largest liqueur bottle ever seen. It was as large as one of the jars in which the robber captain hid his forty thieves, although of course it was of glass and somewhat narrower about the neck. From this he poured an invisible liquid into tiny thimble glasses which stood before each guest. Kincaid rose in his place and again silenced the company.

"I give you the toast of my lost boy who has come home!" he cried, and great tears sizzled down his cheeks. This was the signal for all present to indulge in a sentimental scene. They all wept copiously. Several left their places to embrace Mansie. Old Kincaid brought out a red spotted handkerchief and loudly blew his nose. Mr Woodburn suddenly appeared out of nowhere with the redhead on his arm and placed a salver full of gold pieces in front of Mansie. "It is by express wish of the directors!" he said and withdrew backwards, bowing. The redhead seemed to want to stay with the salver, but Kincaid brought them back to the point by shouting, "Ladies . . . gentlemen . . . control your natural emotion! The toast! Let us honour the toast!"

Mansie was deeply touched. How they all love me, how they all value me, how they all honour me, he said to himself. What nice people! Not like some aloof, starchy and correct types I could name!

All the men drained their glasses at a draught, the healthy barman placing his foot on the tablecloth and sending his crystal goblet to smithereens on the floor as soon as it was empty. On the piano Dr Plumdough struck up "For he's a jolly good fellow!" and immediately

170

afterwards broke off into a splendid fugue on the theme. The point and counterpoint coiled round Mansie's brain, and the room seemed to become even darker. All at once he was aware of old Kincaid at his elbow.

"Let me join you, my boy!" he whispered. "All this is a ghastly bore, isn't it? We'll shake them off in due course and make a night of it together. But the duties of a host, you understand —"

He drew a chair close to Mansie and lit a nine-inch Havana cigar.

"I am going to give you a few tips," he went on, "the fruits of my large experience, and I suppose of my nature and instincts. I will put happiness on this earth well within your reach. You haven't been very happy till now, have you?"

Mansie admitted he had not.

"For example, your childhood — can you honestly maintain that it was enjoyable? Can anyone? Doesn't it resemble emergence from some filthy anaesthetic after an operation? One is sick all the time and, as one comes round, conscious of more and more excruciating pain. And the army . . . weren't you miserable, herded with all those stinking vulgarians?"

Mansie had never been so understood.

"Ah!" said old Kincaid with a sigh. "How I pity youth for its stupidity and lack of expertise; its desperate attempts to find contentment in toeing the line. Isn't that old woman Thin a drab and tiresome creature, with her ideals of respectability? How a fellow like you can have stood it, I don't know! But really, my dear boy, there are limits to what can reasonably be expected in the line of filial duty. The animals make short shrift of that bond, and we can't very well understand ourselves unless we accept the fact that we are only somewhat peculiar animals. But animals, my dear lad, animals — clever animals, I agree, who find the fugues of my friend Plumdough more satisfying than the croaking of bull-frogs in the sodden marshes. Poor old Thin, with her mops and her brooms and her passion morality — how could a fellow like you remain tied to her apron strings? And here, if you'll forgive an old man the presumption, I want to address a few very serious words to you. Men have an Œdipean tendency to marry their mammas, and when I see you floating about with that — oh I do not deny it — that foamy little damsel, I have fears that you may be on the brink of a grave mistake. Not an irreparable mistake, of course. It has always been possible for a man to break away from a woman, and nowadays it has become in some ways easier, though perhaps not in others. But that takes time. I recommend you to avoid that particular crevasse. I expect you'd hardly believe it, but your mamma was once not a little like that child. But I didn't make that mistake. Love 'em and leave 'em, my son!"

He leaned back to inhale the smoke of his cigar and emitted such a puff of smoke that it became hard even to make out the table and the faces of the other guests. Mansie had, however, an impression that they were all leaning forward in an eager attempt to see and hear. He was flattered that old man Kincaid should have singled him out in this way towards the end of the meal, and that they should have this private arrangement to be rid of the others. Kincaid leaned close to him.

"Tell me, with complete frankness, what gave you first taste of happiness in the vale of tears?"

Mansie did not take long to find the answer.

"The malacca cane!" he said.

Kincaid seemed pleased.

"Ah, my old cane! A beauty, isn't it? I can feel it now in my hand. I had it from my lusty progenitor. I sometimes think it may once have been Merlin's wand. My lawless vitality, my overriding manhood — I think you have inherited those along with the cane. Well, well, my boy, that is no more than the overture. You have sampled the joys of confidence, of mastery, of maturity. But they are no more than the first shivering rays of the sun on a February day. You are on the threshold of spring. My boy, I can promise you a splendid summer and a mellow autumn! The whole world was my oyster. I am in a position to pass on to you the sum of all knowledge, which is how to prise it open."

Mansie was carried away by the indefinite but glowing picture.

"Then tell me," he said. "I am listening and will forget nothing."

"You have heard the word selfishness lightly used, have you not?" replied Mr Kincaid, drawing back a little as if the time were not quite ripe. "And always, I dare lay a small wager, in a derogatory sense. It has become the word which the feeble apply to the vital who sweep them from their path, ravish beauty from their arms, press to the front row in the procession of life, and by their superior gifts show up all the rest as inadequate, drab, grey. Philosophers will admit that all life is a dark chamber in which one may develop and enlarge the glowing print that is oneself. They will prate of the individual. Yet as soon as one man steps out in front of the herd, their hands are up in horror. The first lesson, my boy, is not even to hear their pious mutterings."

"And then?"

"Yes, then —"

Old Kincaid studied him for an interminable moment, then became business-like.

"Turpin!" he called. "Fetch the Visitors' Book! Confound you! Why can't you have it ready! I'll thrash you till you squeal!"

Poor Turpin had the book on the table almost before the outburst was ended. It was a handsome volume, bound in morocco with gilt lettering and edges. Kincaid opened it at a fresh page and drew a gold fountain pen from his pocket. He held it out to Mansie.

The cigar smoke was swirling closer and closer about his ears as he reached out to take it. He could scarcely make out anything except the cayenne face of old Kincaid close to his, the gold pen and the virgin page of the album. But he never touched the pen, for the silence was torn wide by a long blast on a ship's siren. Kincaid leapt to his feet and at once the smoke began to rise towards the ceiling. Through it Mansie could see three figures emerging. They were Magnus Thin, in the uniform of first mate of the Inchcolm and Inchmickery Steam Packet, Mrs Thin in her working clothes, with her sleeves rolled up and a broom held like a halberd, and Myrtle clad in a chiffon nightdress. She looked like a stripling goddess, as beautiful as an advertisement in an expensive magazine.

"Thin, this is an intrusion," said Kincaid, with savage calm.

"Kincaid, you have crossed my path once too often," replied the first mate.

"Sir, I ask you to leave — at once!" snapped Kincaid, pointing to the door.

Thin looked at him for a moment before replying, in a quiet voice, "Get below decks, you cur. I warn you, if you do not comply, it is mutiny!"

It had been the calm before the storm. Without warning Kincaid seemed to lose control of himself.

"Throw him out, Turpin! Chuck him in the street! Make mincemeat of him!" he shrieked, his face ruddy with apoplexy. Turpin sprang on the first mate, who side-stepped like a professional boxer and caught him a pile-driver on the point of the jaw. Turpin fell senseless.

For a split second Thin and Kincaid eyed one another, then all hell was let loose. Kincaid turned tail and made for the door, with Thin after him. There were screams and roars as they passed from sight. Madame Désirée had risen from her place. She now set furiously upon Mrs Thin, who defended herself stoutly with the broom. Mansie would have gone to his mother's assistance, but at that stage Dr Plumdough rose from the piano stool, threw Myrtle over his shoulder and started to clamber out of a window. Then it was that Mansie found the use of his limbs. He flew to the rescue. It was lucky for the minority that their enemy were too divided to deploy their forces against them, for Brother Jeroboam had evidently nourished a passionate jealousy of long standing for Brother Gamaliel, and was trying to crown

Sister Dinah with a cut-glass vase, impeded by the healthy barman. Only Mademoiselle Julie remained calm. She sat smoking a cigarette in a long holder, her eyes narrowed to mere slits. Even when the table-cloth was swept off, she never moved a muscle.

In the window Mansie and Dr Plumdough were enjoying an epic struggle. Mansie felt that he was not doing himself justice, for the Mus.Doc. seemed to be made of cotton-wool and the air was as hard to part as treacle. His style was further cramped by his intense desire not to wrench off Myrtle's nightie in front of the organist. No such scruples weighed with his opponent. As he swayed on the ledge there was a rip, Myrtle screamed, and the Doctor, with Mansie on top of him, fell headlong to the gravel path below. That was the last Mansie knew of the battle of the Osiris.

When he came round, he was lying on top of his bed at No. 2 Bleachfield. His mother was bending over him, with her broom in her hand.

"What nonsense is this?" she asked with asperity. "You don't say you haven't had off your clothes all night! And the window wide open too! You'll catch a double pneumonia at the least! I have to be out early this morning, so don't drop off again. You can just make your own breakfast for once. And look at that good-for-nothing cane! What is it doing here in your bedroom? Oh, how I hate that cane!"

She swept out, banging the door. Mansie never remembered seeing her in a worse temper.

CHAPTER
FOURTEEN

The Point of Granton Breakwater

The first action which Mansie took was to wash in cold water. He felt frowzy enough for toadstools to grow on him, and every time he thought of the events at the Osiris on the previous night he had the terrors. Was Myrtle safe? How had she returned without her nightie? The pearly light of morn induced him to hope that sanity might have returned to the world, but he had to be sure about Myrtle. To call on Mrs Bremner at that hour of the day almost deserved the label of immorality and could not be seriously considered. That was when he remembered that Myrtle slept in the room below the Thins' parlour. He took a length of twine and affixed to the end of it a note which read, "Are you all right?" Then he opened the window and cautiously paid out the string till the folded paper was level with Myrtle's window. By clever wiggling he was even able to make it scrape her window-pane.

Before long he heard the window raised and a fair white arm was extended. He paid out more twine so that she might take the note into her room without difficulty.

In due course the arm appeared and released a reply. Mansie feverishly hauled it up.

"Yes. But had disturbed night."

Mansie hastily wrote "Love" and let down the paper. In a short time it returned with the message, "Much love." That was gratifying. But Mansie's mind returned to the original worry. He wrote hard.

"How do you mean disturbed? You really are all right?"

The string disappeared for a space, Myrtle not being of a literary turn. But in due course he dredged up the following:

"Mean kind of restless. What's the matter with you?"

To which Mansie replied, "Very anxious about you. What about a walk?"

"Are you crazy? Where to?" wrote Myrtle.

"To Granton Breakwater. Sea air much recommended for tonic effect."

"Still think you crazy. But am on. Give me ten mins."

In ten minutes to the second Mansie was on the landing below, swinging his malacca cane. The door opened and Myrtle stole out. She kissed him with some reluctance because of her make-up and they descended the stair in hand.

"Why were you restless?" fished Mansie.

"I suppose because I have such very funny dreams," said Myrtle. "Somehow I imagine you don't have any dreams at all, Mansie, but I lie and dream the whole night through. Such daft things, too! I would be ashamed to repeat to you some of the things I dream. My mother says it will all stop when I'm married. If I ever do marry," she added.

"Did anything peculiar happen in the dream?" he pursued.

"Oh lots! But what am I telling you? I wouldn't repeat the half that happens to me in dreams. Funny, I must have caught my foot in my nightie, for when I woke up it was ripped in two and hanging off my back. It was a good chiffon one too. Fancy me telling you an intimate detail like that!"

"How did you get home? Did you fly?"

Myrtle looked at him closely.

"What a funny boy you are," she observed. "I always said there was more to you than most people would admit, and I can see I'm right. How did you guess? Of course I flew. That's the kind of dream I have. I fly quite a lot in my dreams. And I shouldn't have cared to have to walk through the streets in — in my condition."

The cool grey sky was changing to a distant blue and the birds sang gaily in the Botanic Garden. Two magpies flew across the street, on which no traffic had yet appeared. One or two boys were trundling carts laden with crates of milk bottles, and a girl was delivering newspapers. They walked along step for step as if they were behind a pipe band. The air had suddenly made them feel like athletes who I could never site.

Mansie had a weight on his mind. He felt obliged to make a clean breast of his personal affairs to Myrtle. Why she should be entitled to this privilege was not quite clear, but he wished to keep accounts with her straight. They had reached Goldenacre before he was able to summon up enough courage.

"Myrtle," he said, "I have a painful confession to make."

She did not appear to be as stirred by the announcement as he felt his news would justify. She merely pressed his hand and smiled, as if his saying could never be so wonder fully important as his being.

"I am sorry to have to tell you I am a bastard."

She frowned, and withdrew her hand.

"Mansie, I wish you wouldn't use that word. It isn't very nice."

"I don't mean to be rude. But it happens to be true."

"I'm not thinking of myself, though it's not a word I care for at any time. I'm thinking of your mother. It isn't a nice thing to say about her and I'm surprised at you. Oh, I know she thinks I'm flighty and a bad influence on her precious boy, but she's a woman, the same as I am."

Mansie was both touched and annoyed by her stand.

"I am making no reflection on my mother —" he began, she cut in with a swift, "I should hope not!" and threw him off his course.

But he had to explain. He began again:

"You see, for years she told me about my father, and then I found he was totally different. I thought he was decent, considerate, a real gentleman, something of a hero in fact. Only the other day I discovered quite by chance that he was selfish, sensual and ruthless."

Myrtle suddenly took his hand again, and smiled at him fondly.

"You dear pet," she said. "I can understand her difficulty, poor soul!"

Mansie began to be incensed by her seeming lack of comprehension.

180

"But what right had she," he argued, "what right on the face of this earth had she to pretend that my father was a good man, when really he was a perfect rip?"

"I should have done exactly the same if I had been in her shoes," Myrtle replied firmly. "She would have to hold him up as an example to you, and it would hardly do to hold up a perfect rip. She would have been a very poor mother to you if she had. And you seem to have found out the truth to your own satisfaction, so I don't see what harm has been done."

"I just don't understand it," said Mansie.

"Well, I do perfectly," Myrtle chirruped, "and what's more, I see it all over again in you. I always thought you were such a nice, quiet person, but the second dance you took me home from, Mr Thin, gave me quite a different slant on your personality!"

She said this in an arch and brilliant way, which somehow flattered him beyond any compliment he had ever heard. Myrtle went on.

"Just now, by the cool light of day, I want my nice, dependable Mansie, but there are other times — oh, I don't know whether I ought to tell you — when I want a perfect devil, compelling, masterful, devouring. Oh Mansie, I couldn't even begin to love a man if he hadn't that devil in him and didn't frighten me sometimes."

This is worse than old man Kincaid's party, thought Mansie. All that happened in the Osiris last night was crystal clear and tediously logical compared with what is now taking place on the road to Granton. He tried the high ironic key.

"Are you by any chance suggesting that I had two fathers instead of the more normal quota of one?"

Myrtle was not put out.

"I suppose most people have two fathers," she said. "At least two. I expect some have four or five. But a mother who is taking her job seriously will naturally choose best to tell her child about. Anyway, when you were a mere infant, how could you have taken in the idea of the old rip? You simply couldn't have understood! It wouldn't have meant a thing!"

Myrtle seemed to be getting much the best of the argument, for he could not pin down her pertinent and feminine illogicality. He must have looked worried, for she said kindly, "Don't make such heavy weather of it. What does it matter now? It's all in the past!"

"Indeed it is in the past!" cried Mansie. "The key of my nature is there in the past, in the blood and the bone of the men who made me! Don't you know that all men itch for self-knowledge?"

"I don't know whether it's wise that they should have too much of it," Myrtle observed judicially. "I suppose you think that if you knew all your beginnings, you would know how you would act, how you must act! That would be very dull. Also, I think it would be terrifying. If I knew what I should do all the time, I think I should jump off Granton Breakwater. But take your own case. It's much better fun wondering whether the saint or the sinner will take the upper hand."

"I resent the way mother tried to take me in!" cried Mansie, determined not to be smothered.

But Myrtle was ready for him.

"Now really, Mansie," she replied, with the merest hint of impatience. "Men are not very good at understanding, are they? What right have children to expect to know all the secrets of their parents?"

"I think they have a considerable right!" exclaimed Mansie with spirit.

"Well, I don't!" said Myrtle. "And I don't think you will either when you have some children of your own. These confessions don't do any real good. They just leave people more confused and embarrassed."

That is certainly true, thought Mansie. I don't know how I shall ever look my mother in the eye again.

By this time they had reached the ugly little coaling port in the basin of which sat yachts, like spotless ladies who found themselves obliged to travel in a workmen's train. Mansie and Myrtle could not argue any more, because they had to clamber up the rough sloping side of the Breakwater and then pick their way over the huge blocks of stone composing it. The breeze was fresh over the sea, blowing up the Forth Estuary and bearing the odours of the gas-works away in the direction of Glasgow. The islands of the Forth, which had seen Sir Patrick Spens sail for Norway, were rising out of the haze, and across the firth the sands of Aberdour were beginning to glint in the morning sun. The only ship upon the face of the waters was a cargo vessel of the Inchcolm and Inchmickery Steam Packet Company which was heading for the Port of Leith from the north, accompanied by a cloud of sea-birds like a swarm of midges. Solan geese were flying overhead on their way

183

home to the Bass, and sometimes these gannets dived into the water with a splash like a tiny bombshell.

When they reached the point of the Breakwater, they stood for a long time hand in hand, first looking their fill at the hills and coast-line of Fife, then coming nearer home, until they found out the interminable beauty of the green waves and could work out the patterns for which the seaweed and the barnacles had been striving year after year. Mansie felt full of a powerful relief which he could not explain. Last night the confusion of life had seemed inexhaustible; this morning, although he did not really understand one whit more, it appeared straight-forward and full of promise. And his heart soared in an unreasonable way, as if evil were banished to the distance, and good was all about him, close at hand.

It was the moment Myrtle had been waiting for.

"Mansie," she said, turning the lamps full on, so that the wattage of the morning sun sank back to nothing by comparison. "Mansie, my dear, I have been very worried about you."

Mansie might have felt a momentary twinge of annoyance that so many people should be interested in him, but instead he was almost overwhelmed by the thought that he was a source of anxiety to this outstanding example of God's handiwork. At that moment she reached out and took the malacca cane from his nerveless grip.

"Yes, dear, I'm worried, and I have taken a great dislike to this cane. I'm bound to say it's what first made me look at you twice, but lately it seems to me to be getting out of hand. It will get you into serious trouble yet."

Maybe you're right, Mansie was thinking.

"A little of it was quite a good thing," she went on, "but the more you give way to it, the more it seems to get above itself. I know one thing. I could never marry a man who took pride in a cane like that."

This was a facer, although Mansie had always known that one day the cane would bring about a crisis. He had become deeply attached to it. Yet he could not deny that it frightened him too. It had gained power over him with truly alarming speed and now behaved with impetious uppishness. Mansie knew that he had begun to fear the cane because it was beginning to take the place of will and reason. Yet when he recalled how much the cane had done for him, how ungrateful that seemed!

"I could never dream of marrying a man with a cane like that," Myrtle repeated.

Mansie felt that it was all fatally easy — and held an irresistible charm. If he made her a present of the cane, she would marry him; he would run into no more of these unexpected and trying adventures; he would not be possessed by this haunting dread lest in the end of the day the cane should prove his ruin. By one act he could solve every problem.

"All right," he said. "Have it! It's yours."

"Do you really mean that?"

"Of course!"

"And everyone's entitled to do what they like with what's given to them?"

"Naturally."

Myrtle let go his hand. Exerting every ounce of her strength, she whirled the malacca cane twice round her head and hurled it far out to sea.

"Oh!" gasped Mansie, and there was a sob of true regret in his voice. The dear old malacca cane, which had led him through the gates of the mysterious world, and had taught him all he knew! The dear old malacca cane, which had procured him content in love, and advancement in his profession! This was how he had used it. Delilah had nothing on Myrtle, of that he was sure. The cane would sink to the bottom of the Forth, with the spars of ships and the oyster shells and the heavy blunt instruments discarded by-passing murderers. A foul, a casual, an unworthy end for such an *objet d'art*!

"Well, that's the end of the dear old cane," cooed Myrtle in a satisfied voice. "I was sorry to have to do it, but it was for your sake, so I had to be strong."

She was looking out to sea, at the spot where the cane hit the water. A frown crosssed her brow.

"It's floating!" she said. "I could have sworn it would sink, with all that weight in the head!"

Instantaneously and inwardly, Mansie rejoiced. He nearly fell in the sea from looking. There, sure enough, was the malacca cane, a little submerged at the knob, but bobbing along quite happily on the flowing tide. Now that the cane no longer threatened him so closely with a life of uproar and riot, he was much relieved to know that it was still there, like the fun in life which one does not desire to have the whole time. He even felt a delicious shiver of fear — as he imagined how one day he would be walking along the shores of the Forth, perhaps at some excessively innocent hour like three o'clock on Sunday afternoon, and there among the rocks would be the malacca cane, waiting to greet him, ready once more to direct his steps in new and unmapped paths. When the skies were drab and drear, that was when he expected to find it. But of course, if he married Myrtle, they would never be. In that event he hoped the cane might fall into the hands of someone else, and prescribe the shock treatment which had been so efficacious in his own case.

The survival of the cane had curiously affected Myrtle. She hung closely to Mansie's arm, as if the little gram of uncertainty made him doubly precious. As if to reassure her, he clasped her to him, and they tottered on the edge of the Breakwater in a dizzy and adhesive kiss, until the skipper of a trawler, apprehensive for their safety, sharply sounded his siren.

"Let's go back. They'll be wondering what has happened, to us," Myrtle said, glancing at the trawler in annoyance.

"Besides," put in the practical Mansie, "I am quite hollow with hunger and I expect so are you."

As they walked home they said little. For one thing that is quite a stroll. But if he was not talking, Mansie was thinking, turning over and over again the story of the curious experiences into which the malacca cane had led him. With the persistence that distinguishes men from the rest of creation, he was trying to reduce them to an equation to which he could refer as a well-proven principle in ordering his future conduct. But the final formula eluded him.

The one person he had left out of his calculations was Mrs Thin. This singular omission burst upon him as he strode along. Her innocence, her abandon, her reticence, her dour courage — how had he come to overlook her virtues? How did it never occur to him that they might have a bigger say in his life than the infallibly perfect behaviour of the first mate or the sensualities of old man Kincaid? To think that, through her, he had a grandfather who was a patriarch and who had gone round the bend! To think that his auntie had eloped with a seal and that his first cousins were swimming the Atlantic! Neither the Kincaid nor the Thin connection could provide anything quite up to that.

He was back where he began, a dispiriting conclusion. Yet as soon as he reached it, he knew it to be false. He would never be back where he began, or if he did come to rest there, it was only after passing through several universes and storing the knowledge of them in his mind. He could not look at this quest for the secret of his nature as wholly fruitless. The mystery lay unsolved, but his eyes were opened. He knew that he had grown up.

Many a time would he kick against the restraints, many a time would he sigh for the fit of the malacca cane into his palm and the excitement of following it whither it led. But against that there was Myrtle. He glanced and saw her, marching there by his side, her cheeks rosy with such strenuous exertion in the salty air.

He had to thank the cane for Myrtle, and now she had cast it away. He did not mind.

ISIS publish a wide range of books in large print, from fiction to biography. A full list of titles is available free of charge from the address below. Alternatively, contact your local library for details of their collection of ISIS large print books.

Details of ISIS complete and unabridged audio books are also available.

Any suggestions for books you would like to see in large print or audio are always welcome.

ISIS

7 Centremead
Osney Mead
Oxford OX2 0ES
(01865) 250333